LARRY FRANCIS

Belief
in the
Great Gear After

Time & Place Prize Publishing
Chicago

No actual beliefs were harmed in the making of this book.

Text set in Garamond

A Time & Place Prize Publication
Chicago

ISBN — 13: 978-0-69-235510-7

For Patrick Edward Daley

Belief

in the

Great Gear After

Let what you say be simply 'Yes' or 'No';
anything more than this comes from evil.
Matthew 5:37

A BIG WHEEL

On a mild midmorning, one winter weekday, in a monochrome conference room between cinderblock walls, somewhere between east and west, north and south, a man in a tailored charcoal suit with perfect white teeth stood at a podium and cleared his throat. The man was known as the Ear. And the Ear believed in himself. He believed in his calling. And he believed that the words he was about to utter were the living truth.

The Ear spoke in a pleasant baritone with an inborn confidence, the kind of confidence that comes from trust funds and conviction. He spoke of a new world. He spoke of transformation. He spoke of change. He spoke of the future. A very bright future. For them all.

For. Every. Single. Person. In. This. Room.

The Ear, believe it or not, spoke of gears.

Eleven full-time employees—senior engineer Lars Kilgore was missing, as usual—of the American

Gear Enterprise (AGE) sat and listened to the Ear. Some believed what they heard, some did not. Either way, the Ear was their new boss, the new chief executive officer, and he was talking about *his* vision of *their* future.

The Ear was a new addition to the AGE family. He had been hastily hired after the sudden departure of the former CEO, Darryl Lawrence. Lawrence, who had served as boss for almost twenty years, left without warning. At the tail end of a strategy meeting he rose, muttered that he couldn't 'do it anymore' and strode out. And that was that. Things change rapidly sometimes. One cog moves another. Or so it seems. It's all a matter of ratios. A month later the smiling, sanguine former COO of StunTek (a software firm specializing in non-lethal assault weapons) was chosen as AGE's new leader.

The Ear wasn't called the Ear when he was offered the position. He accepted it under another name. The otological nickname was earned his first day on the job. As a matter of fact it happened during his introductory address. Sometimes things do change rapidly.

I understand that I am new to your distinguished industry. I am an outsider. And, believe you me, this lack of experience is humbling. But I come here, to AGE, to make it better, not different. I am not here to advocate change for change's sake. I am here to help. I am here to *learn* as well as to *teach*. As such my first mission, then, my very first order of business, will be to listen—really listen—to each and every one of you.

And here, for intensifying emphasis, he pointed to them, slowly, one by one.

I want to hear from you what works and what doesn't. I want to know about your role here and what I can do to make it better. I want *you* to educate *me*. I want you to tell me how to succeed. I will listen to you. That is my pledge. That is my promise. I will listen. You will be heard.

And then he took a pause pregnant enough to deliver the unfortunate nickname.

I want be known as the one who put the *ear* back in gear.

He paused again, this time to let his quip—wittily resounding in his well-coiffed head—register.

And with your help, I will. And together we will institute a new AGE.

No, the Ear's real name, the name printed on his birth certificate, was not the Ear. Fortuity like that would most surely test the credibility of any story, especially a story about belief. His Christian name— for he was a good and faithful Christian, a born-again Christian, in fact—was Paul. The Ear was Paul Chauncey Briar.

Names last only so long. Some don't exist for more than a moment or two. Others fade after a few years, maybe a decade, perhaps an epoch. How many survive a millennium? Two millennia? Like most living things, names have a shelf life. For whatever reason—brevity, absurdity, irony?—the Ear stuck. But would it last longer than the Ass? That's what the Ear had been called at StunTek, a tribute to his uncanny ability to ride and/or kiss the appropriate behinds in his meteoric rise to COO. Or what about the Foot? He earned that one at age seven when Mrs. Jones, a generally unsteady second grade teacher, tripped over the Ear's rather developed and ill-situated left foot and launched into a literal nosedive followed by a colorful, unforgettable, and age-inappropriate rant cursing the size and position of the offending, offensive appendage.

In any event, as he addressed his new employees, the Ear wasn't contemplating anatomy or salty, old Mrs. Jones. He had never much cared what others thought of him and he hadn't thought about Mrs. Jones in more years than he cared to count. The Ear was thinking about gears. The Ear was thinking about providence. The Ear was thinking about a glorious future. And those before him, sitting and listening, fidgeting and whispering, were to be part of the grand plan. Well, some of them anyway. My minions, he thought. And then he humbly but fittingly corrected himself. No, we are all merely God's pinions.

The Ear was thirty-three years old and convinced that he was on a holy mission. He believed Christ himself had sent him to AGE, the CEO appointment but a small part of the Lord's glorious plan. The Ear believed with all his heart and all his faith that he had been chosen to resurrect the ailing American gear industry and usher in a new, more perfect, world in general. He believed in his destiny. He had been chosen. It was his fate. It was his belief. The Lord had spoken. And the Ear had heard.

The American Gear Enterprise (AGE) was founded in 1916 by a calloused handful-plus-one of the largest gear manufacturers in the United States. The original members were on the whole named unoriginally in hometown fashion: the Pittsburg Gear Works, the Harrisburg Manufacturing Company, the Philadelphia Gear & Machine Company, and the Cincinnati Gear Cutting Machine Company. The two radical founding members not christened after cities were the Kimball Company from Chicago and the Lake Erie Gear & Machine Company based in Toledo, Ohio

AGE was created when the Kimball Company gathered the others together to discuss developing technical standards for non-metallic gearing, an exciting beginning. Their first official annual meeting was held in Pittsburg on April 4, 1917, the same day the United States entered World War One. The owner-industrialists agreed at that meeting that there was money in patriotic cooperation, lots of money. Nearly one hundred years later AGE would boast four hundred members, stretching from Mexico to Canada.

Thrilling technical standards and world wars long since settled, the twenty-first century team at AGE performed three largely perfunctory functions for its dues-paying members:

Staging an annual gear manufacturers' conference to be held in a suitably warm and semi-exotic clime;

Lobbying national lawmakers on the nationalistic importance of gear-related issues; and,

Providing ad hoc, ad hominem, ad infinitum gear design consulting as requested and contracted.

The Ear had been at the helm of AGE for two exiguous weeks—nine work days to be exact—and he was already making his second formal speech to the assembled full staff. For an ear, he talked a great deal.

I see opportunity, he said. There are amazing opportunities here, people. Yes, wonderful, fantastic opportunities. We can make AGE great. I know we can. I have faith. And you should too. We can do so much more than we are now doing. So much more. There is tremendous room for growth, for value-add. But we have to be smart about it, don't we?

The Ear dipped his hairless chin in a slight nod and his retirement-aged assistant, Magda, lurched to her feet bearing a neat stack of thick, red and white, embossed folders. As Magda passed out the packets, the Ear paused and displayed his bright, white teeth in a calculated smile until the commotion of the unexpected paper presents waned.

And to be smart about it we need a plan, he continued. A clear path forward. And we need ways to measure our collective success. That's the only way we'll know if the plan is working. Right? Right. You have in your hands the outline of that plan. *Our* plan. Go ahead, look at it. That's right. And, beneath each and every ordained step you will see how it will be measured, how we have made everything quantifiable. There is no guesswork. No supposition. See it? Yes, right there. Furthermore—and I'm sure most of you have already noticed—I have assigned someone in this room primary responsibility for each task, every small step in our comprehensive plan. You all have a role to play in the plan. You all have a role in our future. Now, don't worry, we won't be going over every item today. That wouldn't be a very efficient use of our time, would it? Count your blessings. Ha. No, the purpose of our get-together today is to introduce this new way of doing business, to increase your comfort level. Welcome to the world of metrics, ladies and gentlemen! Welcome to the twenty-first century! It's a quantifiable meet and greet, if you will. Out with the old, in with the new. So take some time and look it over. This is your work bible. Study it. Learn it. It may seem strange now, but, in time, I am sure you will come to rely upon it and to love it.

The Ear grinned. Magda applauded as if her paycheck depended on it. He dipped his chin again and she stopped, her fingers converging on the large blue stone hanging from her neck. He wasn't quite finished.

Ladies and gentlemen, mankind is at a crossroads. This is a historic moment. We have tools and knowledge that our predecessors, our forefathers, could only dream of. It is our duty to put them to good use, to employ them intelligently. And with the new materials and new information come new responsibilities and new messaging. We need to change with the times. It is the twenty-first century. Now, this does not mean that we are abandoning our core business. No, quite the contrary; our annual conference, our yearly trip to the Hill, and our consulting function will continue to be at the heart of what we do—the soul, if you will, of our mission. But our soul will be stronger—we will be stronger— because everything will be results-based. Metrics shall be our new mantra. We are entering a new AGE people. And all must convert. No more apologies. No more ambiguity. No more excuses. We have a new message to spread. Metrics! Results! One truth! People, AGE needs saving. It needs rebirth. And we are the ones chosen to deliver it. This is our destiny.

Magda rose on her short, thick legs and applauded. The Ear smiled when her applause proved contagious.

A girl, for she was hardly more or less than that, dressed in black, sitting in one of the swivel chairs in the back row, near the door, did not clap. She did not join her colleagues' Kumbaya. She was not impressed. She was no sycophant, no toady. She was made of material unfit for a disciple. She was, however, respectful; she was polite. An affected smile belied her beliefs. She wore her sneer on the inside.

A tyro tyrant. They're all the same, thought the pretty young girl in black. She scanned the packet looking for her name. It's got to be here somewhere. I have to be responsible for something. Then she found it. Sobchak. Yes, there. On page nine and . . . nowhere else. One lousy thing? One? she asked herself. Christ, Gwen the receptionist has at least three, she noted. One? She flipped through the packet a second time to make sure she hadn't missed anything. She hadn't. The Ear's grand crusade, his rousing call for a new AGE, had left her holding a token sword. Not even a sword; he'd left her a token knife, a dull butter knife. He had made her responsible for nametags. Conference Nametags. And that was all. That would be her contribution to this new era, to this new age of metrics, to the twenty-first century. Ensuring the uniformity, quality, and use of all conference nametags. How challenging. In the measurement column she read that she would be judged on three separate performance criteria: price, popularity, and participation. Nametags? That's it? That about figures, she thought. In with the new, out with the new. It's symbolic, a message. A sign. The beginning of the end. Fine by me. He wants me out. Oh well, I don't blame him.

The young pretty girl in black, the only AGE employee in attendance who wasn't applauding, just happened to be recently departed CEO Darryl Lawrence's niece. She had been at AGE for less than a year. She reported to the conference director as his executive assistant and didn't much like working, didn't really care for the job, but was too proud to be poor. She had to do something. People work. That's what they do, she told herself. But in her heart she considered herself an avatar, a shadow, definitely ill-suited for office work. Her coworkers kept a respectful distance and called her Sobs, either because of her last name or because her all black wardrobe and demeanor made her look like a perpetual mourner. Sobs didn't care. She secretly enjoyed the nickname.

Sobs was handed the job at AGE straight out of high school, some sort of sibling expiation, she assumed. When her uncle left—without a word to anyone, even her—she lost her protector, her cushion, and her small sense of entitlement. She became expendable. And now she was a target, a liability, a challenge to the new chief's authority. That is how she saw it. Him against her. What difference does it make anyway? she thought. This place blows.

Welcome to the new AGE. A new AGE for everyone! thundered the Ear. Applause swelled to fill the small room. They clapped. The American Gear Enterprise employees clapped. But not all clapped because of the speech or because of the plan. Some clapped out of deference. Some clapped out of decorum and habit. Some were trying to convince themselves that they believed. Others applauded the Ear while wishing him away. Some were only playing a part. Some were doing what was expected. Some feared for their jobs. One or two truly believed in the new vision. And so they all—all but one—clapped, because in the end no one wanted to rub the Ear the wrong way.

Nobody noticed—in general people are too often concerned with themselves to notice others—but there was one name left off the plan entirely, elder engineer and meeting truant Lars Kilgore. Born in Copenhagen, the great Dane was the most senior employee in the company's history. There was even a half-believed rumor that he had been at the very first annual meeting in 1917. Actually he had been at AGE a mere forty years during which he had attained the position of consulting executive director emeritus, a title created specifically for him. He was legendary. He was expert. He knew everyone and everything. In the pun-proud gear industry he was known as Gearkegaard. His gear designs were commended, admired and imitated around the world. Gearkegaard *was* gears. Gearkegaard was AGE. And yet, had anyone bothered to look, they would have noticed that the consulting services section was singularly incomplete—TBDs littered the section. To Be Determined. If anything was determinate at AGE it was venerable Gearkegaard. And no one was more determined.

So, had anyone in the room noted, had any of them taken a little time to read between the lines of the great plan, the great path forward, it would have appeared as though the Ear's roadmap for AGE and for the rejuvenation of the entire American gear industry required neither Sobs nor Gearkegaard. The Ear had given them the cold shoulder. He had singled them out by omission. The uninterested and the absent. It was as though these two AGE employees— and these two only—were not to be part of the solution, part of the plan, part of the mission. On paper they were irrelevant, extraneous. Unwanted. It appeared as if the Ear was deliberately amputating the youngest and the oldest parts of the new AGE.

BREAKDOWN

Pharmacology to the rescue: a coordinated alliance of colored tablets. My return, my resurrection, my resumption, whatever you wish to call it, is due primarily to the pharmaceuticals in these two little pills. It's thanks to the medication, that and the fact that I've been able to rest, to sleep, for the first time in many, many, I don't know how many, months. I, for one, do not discount the power of a good night's sleep. Dreams and nightmares are meant for the sleeping mind, not the conscious one. To wake we first must sleep. The tablets then have reawakened me. My brain, my thoughts, and my mind are once more mine. I've retrieved ownership . . . of myself. I am well aware my description is awkward and imprecise but that is the way it feels. I have possession again. I *feel* this to be true, that's a strange idea for me, for anyone I suppose, that one can *feel*, physically feel, mind and thoughts, it's an even queerer idea than the unsettling notion that foreign

16

pharmaceuticals, however powerful, induced this return to—admittedly relative—normalcy.

Now that I can talk, not only talk, I am able to listen too, I can communicate—I can understand— we have much to discuss. I understand that this is not the end merely the commencement and I am not, in acknowledgement of this understanding, I am not asking for immediate release. You have made me too well, too sane, to request such precipitous folly. Furthermore I am well aware I hold little power in this relationship. The room dynamics are enough to confirm this suspicion. My old office had a similar design; the guest chairs featured the same austerity. For the time being I am content to remain here, getting better day by day. I know—rather, I feel—that there is much to do before I am ready. And I assume you too wish my eventual—dare I, at this incipient stage, say inevitable—return to the outside world, a return to full independence, to be as successful as humanly and pharmacologically possible. The symptoms have been controlled and there is much to be done. How much I do not know. I am not yet requesting a prognosis or a schedule. I feel better. And that is enough for now. You and your pills and expertise have helped me and as a consequence have earned my trust and faith, not to mention my gratitude.

Even at its most accurate memory recalls but incomplete truth. Anything I say, anything I *remember*, is by definition a retrospective construction, an event, an image or a *feeling* which may or may not reflect reality, particularly given the circumstances. Whatever a man does is plausible to him at every moment, he justifies it to himself with reasons which in his eyes represent the truth, he proves it to himself logically, and his actions are always justifiable. I cannot explain why I feel this caveat a necessity, yet I feel it appropriate. I feel it is honest. What do I remember of my madness? I recall the diseased period in waxy blots, like thin slices of hardened Swiss cheese. But there are holes in my memory, irregular and random. The story of my insanity, then, is necessarily one of gathering these holes and patching them together into a narrative whole—no pun intended—which all sounds rather meaningless. It's like adding zeroes to zeroes. The sum remains zero. And at the time—had you asked me while I was living it and had I the ability to understand your question—the story would no doubt be altogether different. Therefore in practical terms apart from the patches there is no story, only survival. And yet it seemed normal to me then. Or at least I think it seemed mostly normal. But I was ill. I don't know.

I do know that I couldn't call a halt to the madness. I do know that I tried. I lived in filth. I was sick. I don't know the proper term for my illness— the politically or scientifically correct term—that is somebody else's business. You now tell me I was suffering from psychotic depression. Whatever you call it I was out of my mind. I was crazy, insane, demented, mentally ill. I was sick. I know that now. I hid. I felt I had to hide. I shut myself away in my house. I became an animal. Surrounded by the rotting remains of partially masticated take-out I crouched unable to do anything, unable to bathe, to speak, to function. I did nothing. I was nothing. I forgot to eat for days. Weeks passed, the beast—I don't know what else to call it, an evil presence—boring its way through my brain like a ravenous malignant-toothed blind worm devouring nerves, axons and dendrites, disrupting synapses and neurotransmitters, disabling everything that worked, everything that made me me. I listened to the creature scratching around inside my skull, slithering between the wet folds, erasing my past, changing my future. At times I screamed and slammed my head against the floor in hopes it would stop. It grew fatter and longer, consuming more and more of my personality. I badly bloodied my ears jabbing needles and whatever else I could find into my ear canals hoping to miraculously pierce the relentless insect, an insect that was actually an idea. Imagine piercing an idea with a needle. But to me, then, without the benefit of sertraline and olanzapine, it was an insect, a worm. I was too tired to make it to my bed. I slept, when I was able, when the worm slept, curled on the floor like a dog in its own filth. I slept, when I was able, a few minutes, here or there, days or nights apart, when the worm slept.

Three times—saying this I'm reminded of cock crows, though I am not a religious man—three times the lethargic fog lifted, replaced by a short-lived purblind mania. The first time I tried to check myself in at this very hospital. I improbably made it through the front doors. I made it to the long desk. There was a woman there. She may have been a nurse, or a receptionist, more likely a receptionist, as if I were checking into a hotel. She acted like a receptionist. And nobody nurses anymore. Nurses have become extinct. Even nurses, even *registered* nurses, even registered nurses don't nurse. They manage, don't they? They manage their patients. They manage caseloads, manage medications, manage doses, manage disease. The comforting days of actual nursing are long gone. We manage. We manage the sick, the dying and the living. We manage our money. We are all managers. We manage to get by. Pardon me, the sense of humor returns slowly. The nurse or the receptionist, she told me, she said, if you think that you do not belong here, if there is any question that you should not be here, if you are not one hundred percent positive, then you do not belong and should not be here. Frightened by her doubt I left. The second time—at least I think it was subsequent but it could have been prior—I went to my doctor. I needed help, I told him. He gave me a pep talk, pills and a pat on the back. He said stress could be debilitating. He told me to shower and eat more regularly. It was a simple injunction to look after myself. My doctor said to get away. Travel, he said. It will take you out of yourself, he said. I was unable to leave the permanently soiled round carpet in front of my green armchair and he wanted me to travel, to expose myself to security agents, to board an airplane, to be among others. I fear most doctors don't get much below the surface, present company excepted. Needless to say his medicine did not work. The worm returned more powerful than before. The third time—I am quite certain it was the third time because

20

here I am, our discussion is proof positive—I made it. The nurse or the receptionist, or whomever, opened the inner gates. Yes, here I am. I'm told that you did the rest. Your medicine works. I can talk. I can remember. I am me once more. I am bruised, but I am me. It is as if my—and please forgive the Freudian terminology, I am aware it betrays my age and lack of contemporary knowledge in the field—it is as if my superego went away and has now returned and we— my superego and I—need time to reconnect, to get to know each other again. I suppose that is what we as patient and doctor are doing. You say it's been two weeks since I've been ingesting this particular blend of tablets, two weeks of increasing medication and now I can finally think in spite of this constant alien queasiness. I can finally converse like a rational human being. I can finally be myself again. Two weeks for the sertraline and olanzapine to cleanse my brain of the madness, to defeat the worm.

In 1932 painter Georgia O'Keefe—I minored in art history, it's my secret passion, but perhaps you already know that about me, perhaps you know much more than I think—in 1932 Georgia O'Keefe had a nervous breakdown. They called them nervous breakdowns back then, the nerves could not take it anymore and broke down, shut down. They ceased to function. She ceased to function. She had been working on a mural for Radio City Music Hall, a huge commission. She never finished it. It broke her. For years she was unable to work. She couldn't look at a brush much less pick one up. Like her, I broke down. It's as simple as that. Like her, one minute I was working and the next I wasn't. I quit. I stopped working. I ceased to function.

Trigger? Is that a technical term? For me the word conjures grainy images from old black and white movies, noir detectives with terse threats. I try to picture the man behind the trigger, a man in the shadows in a fedora pulling the trigger with a slow squeeze. But that's all fiction. A trigger is merely a component, just another part of an unthinking purpose-built instrument, a manmade tool meant to make our lives easier and better but in my case delivering destruction in the form of knowledge. There was a trigger but the power lay in the bullet, power over the future, power over men. Yes, I remember the trigger, it was a shopworn phrase transformed into a sentence of prophecy and death. It's a stupid, meaningless, hyphenated phrase that I've heard every day for more than thirty years. I don't remember who in the meeting uttered, that is, pulled the trigger. It doesn't matter. *It's a win-win.* That was the phrase. That was the trigger. *It's a win-win.* It instantly drove me mad. This may not be at all material, but I first heard that phrase in the early eighties—it was coined around then, I believe—and it was the same time we, all of us in the engineering world, were adapting to the machines on our desks. The corporate computer age had arrived. And, win-win, this business school phrase, this instant cliché came in with the ones and zeroes. Overnight we became binary. If/then—either/or—would help us win-win. They are forever paired in my mind. Perhaps it is material after all, significant even. Regardless, the trigger was merely a bit player, an aide-mémoire of the greater issue. The trigger was but another cog reducing me to madness, no more important than any other piece of the machinery. It performed its function. It played its role. But the trigger by itself is, to me, irrelevant. Man is an imperfect engineer. The phrase may have been the trigger, but why I left is something else entirely. First you need to understand the context.

I am reminded of an incident today at lunch. I was alone eating when I was joined by none other than Jesus Christ himself or so he claimed. I must admit the young man was very polite. He was also terribly ill. I looked into the face of insanity. Your treatment, your cure, now allows me to pass judgment. Ah, how quickly wanes the glow of reprieve. The Lord, as he instructed me to address him, was very talkative, preaching how religion had been corrupted and is now being consumed like candy, like drugs, he said. Over and over he warned against the power of placebo. The drug of organized religion: a nocebo, he called it. At one point he stood on the metal table and shouted, *A Messiah who lets himself be crucified. What a thing!* It was clear to me that he needed help but my thoughts—they were again *my* thoughts—my thoughts were how do I get away? How can I rid myself of this madman? Me, someone who days earlier was just as demented, now without a scintilla of sympathy. How quickly we return to our old habits. How inherently dismissive we are. I don't know why I told you this. It was a pointless digression. Please forget it. Where were we? Why did

I wander? There must have been a connection. Right, I remember, because maybe at its core life is a constant search for that hint of a higher idea to which one may submit oneself, ergo religion, ergo Jesus Christ.

Context! The trigger, the inane phrase that activated my insanity, is nothing out of context. The reason human beings are self-deceptive is not that the alternative is horrifying, which it is, but rather self-deception is adaptive—reality and truth and so on are not. We *need* to deceive ourselves to go on. When I lost the ability to self-deceive I lost myself. I ask you—this is an academic question—what precisely did I lose then? The phrase, the trigger, reminded me that I had seen perfection; I had seen the future and the mere existence of that perfection destroyed who I was. The pharmaceuticals coursing through my brain are now helping me adapt, perhaps.

Context. My entire adult life had been about gears. I had designed them, manufactured them, inspected them, sold them, promoted them, anything to do with gears I had done. I was—I am—a gear geek. There are few things—art springs to mind—more beautiful than a well-designed gear assembly. It may sound odd to the uninitiated but there is almost something mystical about an ideal transmission. There are all kinds of gears, from the simple to the complex, from the small to the gigantic, from the deadly to the life-saving. And gears are ubiquitous. If it moves, odds are that gears are involved. Energy is converted and transformed. Gears are in a very real sense transformative. They change what can be done with power. Generating energy is a fairly easy task. Gears harness energy for a purpose. And they are usually inside, hidden, invisible. As a result gears are taken for granted. They are overlooked. They are the unsung workhorses of the mechanical world. And, like people, gears are social, dependent. They need others. They need one another to perform. To work they need to work together, as a team, a synchronous unit. They turn, move and interact in precision. There is— and there is no other word for it—a magic in mechanical torsion. Gears are incredible. At any rate I rose to the top of the gear game. I was the CEO. I was the boss. And I lived and breathed gears. I lived and breathed my work. There was little else.

At this point in my short story I realize that the narrative erroneously leads one toward a classic midlife crisis diagnosis. I assure you that this is anything but classic. First, sixty-two is borderline middle age at best, it isn't old, neither is it quite middle. From my admittedly biased perspective it is the prime of life. It's the meat, the heart, the core of the whole thing. It's the payoff for all one's diligence, one's hard work and one's troubles. And I had everything I wanted. I was content. Second, the root of such common crises, midlife and other, is buried in mortality and I've lived long enough to know not to fear my own mortality. I do not fear death. We return to the void. That is all. I know that in my final moments my past will not flash before my eyes. The past is past. Dead and buried. No angels will sing. My imaginary soul will not escape into the ether. On the other hand, if I'm being honest, I will miss the future, an eternal future I can never know. It will always be speculation. I do not fear my mortality, I do not fear death, but I will miss the future. I will concede as much.

I'm afraid if you wish me to keep talking I must digress once more. I may miss the world, but whether the world will miss me is another question entirely. I wonder what my colleagues, my family, think of me. Do they know my whereabouts? Do they know what happened? Am I missed?

I left without a word. I walked out in the middle of a meeting. *It's a win-win.* I heard that and left. How long has it been? Weeks, certainly. Months? Please don't tell me if it's longer, I am not well enough to tolerate such news. I will not understand. In any case everyone will have moved on. Their lives did not stop; life did not stop. The wheels keep turning. I wonder who took my place. Who now sits in my ergonomic chair in the corner office? If they were smart they will have given the job to Blair. But my best guess is that they were afraid to do so. They would fear giving her that much power. I suspect that is what doomed her chances, that ultimately they were afraid of what they might unleash, the cowards. No, they will search elsewhere, perhaps even outside the gear manufacturing world. They will hire some handsome, silver-haired no-nothing from another company, perhaps he's already a CEO. He's a man who has never accomplished much but his résumé is solid and includes an Ivy League degree or two. He will project stability and tradition. No, that's not it, they will go young. They will want a fresh start. They will succumb to the all-too-seductive belief that new is better; that the world is changing and the world of gears must change with it. Yes, that is what they'll do. They will hire some pretty boy from the Internet, from some inane social media company, somebody who knows nothing about gears but excels in optics, networking, managing expectations, oratory and clichés. Clichés like win-win. I can see him with his full head of perfect hair sitting in my chair, changing things. I'll tell you they won't like it. Presumption will not work. I know things that he will never know, things he will never understand. I can see the future. It is conditional. I can see it. Yes.

BEVEL

Sobs placed the sweating chocolate layer cake in the center of the festooned table. The blinds to the pantry were drawn. No one saw her arrange the paper plates and plastic forks. No one saw her carefully sink a single white candle into the pastry's soft flesh. No one saw her sneak a taste of the dark icing. She looked up at the clock. In ten minutes the room would be thick with others. Another AGE birthday celebration would be underway. Always someone's birthday, she thought. It never ends. When is a surprise not a surprise? Every damn week it seemed. She tried to do the math in her head, but couldn't quite make it work. Fifty-two divided by how many? Twelve? Thirteen?

Today's celebration was to honor her boss, Sam Binder, Director of Conference Services. Sam was turning sixty-one years old. He was a simple man with a loud laugh and a not-so-quiet drinking problem, a man whose voice and belly entered a room well before his feet. He was a happy man. He believed that

28

life was short. Enjoy it while you can, he told Sobs.

Magda was the first to arrive. Gwen followed on her heels and held the door as the others entered in rote succession. After everyone was accounted for, Sobs left to fetch her boss. She found him waiting predictably at her desk and she led him to the pantry without having to say a word.

Surprise, they shouted, as Binder stepped into the room. He feigned disbelief before breaking into a hearty laugh. People liked Sam.

They sang and he made an honest-to-goodness wish before blowing out the tiny golden flame twirling atop the candle. He secretly wished for nothing to change. He wished that he could feel like this always—a bit inebriated amid a sea of friends.

The others wished in silence too: Gwen wished to find Mr. Right, for a lucky third time; Blair Hunt, Director of Congressional Relations, wished she hadn't been passed over for CEO; her assistant, Corey Anderson, wished he wasn't constantly surrounded by such congenital stupidity; Magda Giannis wished magical transport to a romanticized Greece; Tom Healy, Gearkegaard's assistant, wished that his boss could be present to see the happiness on Sam's face; Executive Director of Media & Corporate Communications, Rita Sullivan, wished to complete the rom-com novel she'd been working on for the last eight years; and Sobs . . . Sobs wished for nothing. Sobs didn't wish for things.

The rest wished that Binder would just hurry up and blow so they could have their cake and eat it.

Sam thanked them all, his work family, for the

sincere outpouring of support on this, his special day, another day nearer to death. He roared with laughter at his own joke and half the room noted the waft of whiskey on the wind of his breath.

They ate the cake. They stood and ate chocolate cake with their plastic forks and they talked. They congratulated Sam and they talked, about work mostly, but about other things too.

This'll be my dinner, you know, said Gwen.

Magda scolded her for being too skinny. You are a thistle. Ah, you'll blow away in the breeze. You know, whether they confess to it or not, men do not want to squeeze a bag of bones. They like curves, not angles. Gwen laughed and said that she needed her curves to look good from every angle.

Where's your boss, Healy? asked Corey. Does he even work here anymore? The guy's a ghost. Tom tried to fashion a witty retort, but instead studied Sobs, alone, at the other end of the room.

Seven months in and Sobs still considered herself an outsider, an outlier. And she liked it that way. She kept her distance. She avoided talking to the cake-eaters by cleaning and pretending to check her Blackberry for messages. She also took an extra-long bathroom break, locking herself in the far stall and killing time by separating the two-ply toilette paper. When she returned she couldn't help notice that Corey and Tom—the only two heterosexual men in the room even remotely her age or type—kept looking her way. Men. They're all the same. They see me as they want to see me, as someone else. They don't know me at all, she thought. Her looks and her distrust of others had made Sobs solitary and cynical. It was a matter of survival. Corey slapped Tom on the shoulder and made his way toward Sobs. She watched him approach. She would have preferred talking to Tom. She didn't know why. He had a nice face, she thought. Corey had the looks and confidence of an underwear model. Tom had the looks and confidence of a model train collector. But there was something about Tom. Maybe she wanted to ask him about Gearkegaard. Gearkegaard probably knew where her uncle was? But where was Gearkegaard? She was tempted to ask, but didn't dare. Instead she put on a fake smile for Corey.

The Ear interrupted the festivities long enough to say that he couldn't stay, but wished Sam a happy, happy birthday and many, many more. Then he left, taking Magda with him. It wasn't like the Ear to be so clipped.

Where was Gearkegaard?

The next day, Sam—a little more hung-over than usual—and all the other employees at AGE received a memorandum from the Ear.

FROM: PAUL BRIAR
CORPORATE DIRECTIVE #1
SUBJECT: OFFICE CELEBRATIONS
TO: ALL STAFF
The bedrock of great teamwork is camaraderie. And camaraderie requires socialization. But socializing is a double-edged sword, that is, it cuts two ways. Not enough socializing and we fail to work together. Too much and we lose sight of our mission. So, to that

end, I am herewith issuing Corporate Directive #1 designed to formalize the approval and scheduling of any and all parties, social gatherings, get-togethers, celebrations, festivities, affairs, etc. including, but not limited to anniversary parties, baby showers, birthday parties, bridal showers, graduation parties, holiday parties, potluck parties, reunions, surprise parties, wedding showers, etc. As a result of this directive all requests for the aforementioned must be submitted in writing in advance to the office of the CEO for authorization.

The directive may be read and accessed in its entirety online and hardcopies will also be posted in the CEO's office as well as the staff pantry area.

Thank you in advance.

Welcome to the new AGE,

PCB

(mag)

A bleary-eyed Sam held up the memo and looked at Sobs.

What'd you do, forget to invite him to my party?

Corporate Directive #1 was only the first frog to hop out of the water, as Magda would say. The Ear found that he enjoyed issuing directives. He discovered that such pronouncements could be efficient tools of change, tools that required no perfunctory input from staff.

Corporate Directive #2 codified the proper way to answer outside calls.

You have reached the new AGE. This is (state

your full name and full title). How may I assist you?

Corporate Directive #3 revised the travel policy and lowered per diem rates.

Corporate Directive #4 codified the dress code. Sneakers, sandals and, without explanation, yellow ties were banned.

The Ear was prolific. AGE staff began to expect a directive a day. Some even wagered on the subject of the next one.

Happy Sam Binder went about his duties, schmoozing and cajoling, and ignored the directives; which meant that Sobs ignored them too. Blair Hunt used her weekly one-on-one with the Ear to praise the new directives and suggest her own and so Corey was asked by his boss to come up with ideas for new directives. No one knew if Gearkegaard even read the directives. But Tom followed them to the letter.

Directive #9—the infamous car pool directive— was probably the frog that jumped the shark, the one that croaked too loudly, the one that went too far. Directive #9 was, at its most rudimentary, an unfeigned attempt to satisfy the hallway grumblings so often heard after Directive #1 went into effect. No one liked having their afternoon cake taken away. Staff sulked. They moped. Directive #9 sought to address the need for socializing. The Ear believed he could quell the grousing with a novel idea. And so he wrote another directive. He was, in a very real sense, issuing a directive related to a directive. It was all very post-post-postmodern, very reflexive, very meta. The Ear considered it inspired.

FROM: PAUL BRIAR
CORPORATE DIRECTIVE #9
SUBJECT: MORNING CAR POOL PROGRAM
TO: ALL STAFF

The importance of socialization was highlighted in Corporate Directive #1. The office of the CEO recognizes that the aforementioned directive has led to an unintended reduction in the number of opportunities for non-business-related interaction between staff members. To address this situation, without disrupting our already full workdays, I would like to announce a new car pool program created to ensure quality, non-office time, with one another. The twelve full-time staff members—given the exigencies of the post, the CEO shall not be included—will be divided into three car pools (four people per car) for the morning commute. (Owing to the logistical difficulties inherent in job responsibilities, staff may, should they wish, arrange alternative EVENING transportation.) Geographical propinquity will be considered in establishing manageable and efficient commutes. Car pool configurations may be modified, at the sole discretion of the CEO's office, if practicable. This additional time together will provide an incomparable opportunity to better know your AGE coworkers and, hopefully, forge new bonds and stronger friendships. This program is mandatory. As a result of this directive ALL staff will be required to participate in this exciting initiative. This can be a wonderful opportunity; I urge each and every one of you to please make the most of it.

The program will begin Monday, the 17th. This should

provide everyone sufficient time to coordinate and prepare.

See Magda Giannis in the Office of the CEO for the initial schedule and additional information.

Per usual, this directive may be read and accessed in its entirety online and hardcopies will also be posted in the CEO's office as well as the staff pantry area.

Thank you in advance and happy motoring.

Welcome to the new AGE,

PCB

(mag)

Reaction was mixed. Sobs cringed at the thought. Sam looked for ways to get out of it. Gwen's inner cougar imagined sharing a back seat with Corey. Blair Hunt had her spotless Mercedes detailed. Magda fastened a second periapt around her neck. Tom Healy wished he drove a better car. Rita Sullivan wondered where she'd find the time to listen to her self-improvement CDs. Gearkegaard read the memo, smiled, and promptly forgot all about it.

Car pool one left from Roseland where Rita Sullivan, Sobs, Matt Blanchard, the third member of the lobbying team, and Tom Healy lived. On Monday, car pool one was forty-five minutes late to the office because Rita got lost on her way to Tom's apartment and because they had to stop at four separate coffee houses for four separate orders: one half-caf, one tall black and bitter, one mocha latte, and one tea.

Magda, Tyler Le Goff, who helped manage the annual conference, Blair Hunt and Gearkegaard all living in or near Mount Pleasant were assigned car pool two. Car pool two was only five minutes late on the first day. This was the result of a fifteen minute wait for Gearkegaard who never showed, mitigated by Blair's aggressive—her fellow commuters would say terrifying—driving.

Car pool three departed from Forest Lake and included Corey Anderson, Sam, Siddhartha (Sid) Aziz, a mechanical engineer who worked with Gearkegaard, and Gwen the receptionist. Car pool three was twenty minutes early that initial day of carpooling as they began their commute an hour earlier than necessary after Gwen insisted that a good receptionist never rushes and is never late.

Having survived the first day, day two results were as follows: Car pool three was three minutes early. Car pool two was seventeen minutes late. (Gearkegaard was still MIA.) Car pool one was twenty minutes late for work.

The Ear was not pleased with the mass tardiness, but he understood that change is sometimes painful. They'll get better. A team isn't built in a day, he told himself. They are bonding; they are becoming friends.

On day three, Rita regaled car pool one with her life's story: a suburban rigmarole. Tom would have liked to talk to Sobs but could neither gin up the courage nor find a polite way to arrest Rita. Curbside, car pool two again waited in vain for Gearkegaard. They were late for work as usual. Car pool three argued over radio stations. Gwen wanted love songs, Sam wanted country and Corey wanted NPR.

I believe that the purpose of this excruciating

36

experiment is to be talking and to be getting to know one another, not minding what comes out of the sound system, dead-panned Sid.

On day four it was Gearkegaard's turn to drive. Blair Hunt stood on her porch impatiently tapping expensive and Directive #4-approved, open-toed shoes, waiting and cursing. In the end, late once again, she jumped into her sedan and drove herself to the office vowing revenge. Magda waited too. And then she waited some more. Finally she called for a taxi. Something must've happened to Gearkegaard, she worried. Still in his bed clothes, Tyler watched court television for two and a half hours before calling the office to tell them that Gearkegaard—shock of all shocks!—had never showed and now the hour was impoliticly advanced to make it into the office today.

On day four Tom spoke to Sobs. Marginally out of his way, he picked her up first so she'd sit up in front, beside him, close. He was nervous and, at first, asked too many questions. Sobs answered no more than was necessary.

Before this I didn't even know your name. I mean your last name at least. I figured people called you Sobs because you were always in black and were so quiet, like a mourner, like a widow. I had no idea your name was Sobchak, said Tom. Compared to Healy, that's a pretty cool name. I'm guessing you also have a first name?

Heather.

Huh. Never would've guessed that one. I figured it would be something sadder, like Mona maybe.

Dolorous? she asked.

Yeah, that's more like it, laughed Tom. Sobs almost smiled.

The talking stopped as soon as Rita and Matt got in the car.

On day four Gwen whispered something in Corey's ear and then grabbed a fistful of his upper thigh. The amorous assault caused Corey to swerve into the next lane, bumping into a dirty white van. Sam laughed. Corey shouted at Gwen.

Look what you made me do, you fossil!

Sid sighed and said the car pool idea was the most idiotic thing ever conceived. They were three hours late for work. It was the first time Gwen had ever been late.

The car pool program ended on Friday, the twenty-first day of the month, when Corporate Directive #29 mercifully switched off the ignition. The well-intentioned, but cakeless, program had lasted but a week. It was an unmitigated disaster. The Ear felt he had no choice but termination. Some inspirations are better than others, he told himself. The office celebration restriction was eased.

Gearkegaard—Lars Kilgore—was ordered to appear in the Ear's office at nine o'clock Monday morning. In person. No excuses.

POOR MESH

No. It's ego, nothing more. No one can see into the future. It is and will forever remain beyond our reach. And yet without that promise what would keep us going? Moreover, without such platitudes where would we be? All that is said and done is destined to become ludicrous. Please excuse my dark humor. I find our sessions bring out the existentialist in me. I would blame the medication but I've already decided the medication is only responsible for my new sanity and almost continuous nausea, besides it would not be the full truth.

If I'm not mistaken they used to call this part of the treatment the talking cure. Once more, with the use of an outdated phrase and for the benefit of all, I broadcast my years and ignorance. The fact remains that before it morphed into psychoanalysis or psycho-anything it was known as the talking cure I believe. I've always been fond of that term. *The talking cure.* It sounds benign and anodyne, almost as if talking, as if words themselves were not at the heart of all our breakdowns, psychoses, or whatever you choose to call them, whatever it was I experienced.

They say a therapist's strength of belief in the efficacy of the therapy is a factor in its success. What do you believe, doctor? After all you are a psychiatrist; one who spends his days delving into the psyche. Psychotherapy can improve pharmaceutical response. Have we then returned to the nocebo? Upon uttering the neologism I suddenly remember reading that the word pharmaceutical comes from the ancient Greek meaning sorcery. No, I am not making light of the situation. My attempts at humor belie my fear. I wait in terror for the effects of the medications to lose their power. Perhaps I am stalling. I am nervous. No, I am ready. I am ready to return to my narrative.

As I believe I've mentioned my world had been gears. I worked and that was it. My only outside interest was art. I purchased art books, read about art and visited art galleries when on business travel, but apart from my passion for art my life was work. It was gears. At the time it all seemed normal—it is what people do, isn't it?—my life was my work. Of course I had difficulties like anyone else, life is not perfect. Nor is it always easy. But one endures. At an early age I discovered that success comes from perseverance, everyone can make excuses, it is the simplest thing in the world, but you cannot let life's inconvenient imperfections deter you. One must persist.

Now, today, as I speak from my recently improved medicated perspective, I see that the signs, the unattractive symptoms of my collapse, were all there prior to the win-win trigger. We talked about the trigger but I failed to mention that in the period leading up to it I was already grinding to a halt. I could have been a case study in an abnormal psychology textbook. I was already going mad and I was entirely unaware of the fact. I was depressed. I was under a great deal of stress, concentration had become challenging, and my digestive system was a constant source of pain and discomfort. I lacked energy. I felt guilty and I wanted to disappear. I hid behind doors, both at the office and in my own home. Sometimes, though rarely—at night usually—I felt as if I couldn't catch my breath. I slept less and less. But I continued working. I worked without linking these afflictions to a single malady, without recognizing the signs of impending madness. You say psychotic depression, I say madness. I ignored or regarded as imaginary the symptoms I was incapable of affecting and treated the others with over-the-counter pills or positive thinking. But you can't turn unhappiness into happiness as simply as that, by such blatant tactics.

This is what you want to hear, isn't it? This is the type of reflection that will ultimately lead to my release, is it not? I want this to work so please let me know if I go astray. I believe this is the sort of information I should be sharing. You must be interested in the way I felt as life closed in on me before the rupture. No, as I've explained, at the time it did not feel claustrophobic. I only see that now from the safety of this room with the aid of time and therapy and tablets. But I do see it now, clearly. I did not then. Surely you do not want a detached recitation of the bald facts. Name: Darryl Eugene Lawrence. Profession: engineer and former American Gear Enterprise Chief Executive Officer. Education: BS, MBA. Age: sixty-two. Family: Parents deceased, one sister, one niece. Outside interests: Art. Body Type: Thin. Hair: Thinning. Favorite Color: Purple. Those are facts. They don't tell one much, do they? They were previously known to you no doubt. You know much more than you are revealing. You may already know everything that we will discuss. Perhaps you also know what I am going to say before I do. Regardless, I will say to all and sundry that at the time I did not see the warning signs. I see them now. Is this admission supposed to help me avoid a second episode? Will this prevent another breakdown? I readily concede, despite my affection for the term talking cure, that I don't fully understand the process.

I do understand gears. I can no longer say that I understand them fully, as I once believed with great conviction. Nevertheless I understand gears. I am an expert. They have been my life. Now, gears can do three basic things: they can change the direction of rotational force from one axis to another; they can change rotational speed, and; they can change torque to increase or decrease available power. I can state with a high degree of confidence that pretty much everything mechanical has a gear. And I further aver that if something mechanical has the ability to move, it undoubtedly does so thanks to a gear assembly. But gears are hidden. And nobody wants to know how things work; they just want them to work. I will get to my point in a moment. I am connecting dots. I also understand art. Now I would not profess to the same level of expertise as in engineering. Nor do I mean to imply that I am artistic in any sense of the word. No, I am not an artist. I am an appreciator of art, an art lover. No, I am now arriving at my conclusion. And the conclusion is this: It occurs to me that perhaps the explanation—the underlying attraction or motivation—for my interest in both gears and art is that they *move* me. On a subliminal level could this metaphorical craving for movement, physical and emotional, be a surrogate for my life's lacunae? Well? How is that for self-analysis? A connection such as this must say something psychological about me, about my psyche, about my personality. Is this type of revelation our therapy's aim? Is this attainment? Does it possess the necessary *Eros* and *Thanatos*? Have I made a breakthrough?

No. I assure you my comments were not meant to be impertinent. I was being open and honest. No, I do not think that this is a game. Indeed, on the contrary, I feel as though I am fighting for my life here. However—placing all my cards on the table—I also feel that I am fighting against an opponent who is invisible or, as inconceivable as it may sound, may not even exist. I do not know how to battle against a chimera. I do not know where to direct my energies. This is unfamiliar territory for an overachiever. My instinct, such as it is, is to say what I think you want me to say. I allow you to lead. I imagine that this inclination is fairly common to all psychotherapies, after all, I desire, in the end, nothing less than my discharge. Most caged animals seek a way out. It is only natural that, once feeling better, I work toward that goal. And despite my *voluntary* status I am well aware that without your authorization—in my case let's call it your blessing—I am to remain here just like all the others.

To wit, an attractive blonde woman, a fellow patient, oh, I would estimate in her early to mid-forties, approached me yesterday as I was leafing through the pages of a book. She begged my pardon and then asked—what anywhere else would have been a most peculiar question, but here one quickly gets used to eccentricities—if I was a professional singer. I asked myself whether I had been humming a tune as I flipped the pages of my book. Might I have been softly singing without any awareness? No, I answered. I am not. She did not seem surprised by my response. She looked as though she had expected it. Then she placed her question in context with an explanation that she had once been a singer, one half of a famous vocal duo. Some irrelevant disaster or other had befallen her partner and she had been sent here as a consequence. She said that more than anything else she wished to sing again however she could only do so with a partner. My voice responds only to harmony, she said. So now she spends her days searching for a new partner—*the one*, she calls him, a man, a pure, natural alto—that she may leave this place and be famous once more. She is clearly demented. I wonder, doctor, how long she has been here searching for her perfect partner. How long has she been in this institution looking for the one? She had the deepest blue eyes I've ever seen, they were almost violet. Her story was so sincere, so tragic. Have you ever heard her sing? I am sure professional rules of conduct if not federal laws prevent you from disclosing any information on the young woman. I can't help but wonder if she will search forever, here in this place. It is terribly sad. I see by your expression that you are familiar with the woman . . . and you are not hopeful. It's a pity.

I don't know what to believe. That is the heart of my problem. I want to believe. I know what should be said but I dare not say it. Perhaps I suffer from an unnatural quest for certainty. Perhaps I fear that the madness will return once I say its name. If I say it out loud it will make it real or, even worse, to speak of such an ultimate thing is to damage it, maybe destroy it. These are all possibilities.

Take Francisco Goya for example. I realize, I do, that I, my monologue—and that is, for better or worse, precisely what this is, my monologue—I realize my monologue has become rather pell-mell. Pick your poison. It can either be calculated or spontaneous—in between reeks of fraudulence. Fine. Back to Goya then. The Spaniard was a master at depicting that which could not be uttered, emotions that could not be rationally contemplated. *Saturn Devouring His Son*, one of his 'black paintings' studies this ineffability. Surely you are acquainted with the well-known work. I thought as much. It renders a glaringly insane creature, a man, a god—it is no accident that the god is Saturn, the god of

45

melancholy—driven mad by the act of killing his own son, savagely eating his own flesh and blood. It is an unforgettable image. Critics contend that it illustrates the horrors of Napoleonic warfare or the conflict between youth and old age or that it shows time as the devourer of all things or even portrays the power of God's wrath. But, for me, the painting is about all these things and none of them. It is more primal and more original than that. It is immune to explication. After all, ambiguity is richness. Its power lies beyond words. The work is in the Prado now but it was originally painted on the dining room wall of his house near Madrid. Imagine sitting down to dine in the presence of such a scene. Imagine attempting conversation while this powerful painting wordlessly terrorizes, agitating everyone in the room. This is why I have difficulty speaking about what lies beyond the trigger. Imagine trying to describe something so disturbing that you have difficulty believing it yourself.

Human beings are great believers believing all manner of things. We believe in gods and we believe in devils. We believe in hate and we believe in love. There are times, chosen by us or not, that we believe in each other. Night after night lying in our comfortable beds we believe the sun will come up tomorrow. We believe in a past, a present, and a future—mostly in that order. We believe in bits too small to see and ideas too big to understand. We *all* believe in something. To be human is to believe. Even nihilists have a credo. Through belief we carve out meaning where there is none. And then we climb inside and pretend we are safe. But now, even with the assistance of your medication and therapy, I do not know what to believe. And that is the truth.

While my last word hangs in the air, honesty compels me to report that the group sessions you've suggested seem to me a pointless exercise. I feel they are an ineffectual waste of time. I suspect listening to strangers natter ad nauseam about their offensive problems and fears as I fidget uncomfortably in one of those awful metallic folding chairs will do little to improve my condition. The group setting, a sloppy circle of infernal clanging chairs, implies that we all suffer from the same affliction. It conveys the message that we are all the same. Allow me to propose that this is patently absurd. From a clinical perspective perhaps their tales of woe and madness provide a modicum of commonality, if not entertainment. But my circumstances, I'm sure you would agree, are entirely different, unconventional shall we say. I would not hesitate to use the word unique. Furthermore I perform better by myself. I am goal oriented. In the end am I not responsible for my own recovery? And, finally, the simple fact of the matter is that I like being alone. When I find myself with others I look forward to their moment of departure. The feeling has plagued me my entire life. In general I find others bothersome and boring. I prefer my own company. I fully understand how unbecoming that sounds and that my preferences are not at issue here and I also understand that there is mental health value in community. I do. I am not an idiot nor am I some hermetic misanthrope. I am sociable but, all things being equal, I would rather not be. No, do not confuse the two; our one-on-one sessions are in a separate category. Our discussions—my monologues—are not diversionary; they are necessary. I feel that our sessions are critical to my full restoration. They are different animals entirely. You do not agree. Then I must defer to your expertise and counsel. I trust your judgment. So, if you insist, I will continue with the group sessions for now. But may I formally request a pillow or similar portable cushion to better endure those awful chairs. I might as well make an attempt to reduce the hardship, no pun intended.

That is certainly enough—at least for me and for the time being—about the group sessions. We are nearing our objective here. I feel close to an attempt at describing the indescribable. We are past the trigger. We are almost there and must proceed slowly. It is not without trepidation that I continue. I am unsure what might be let loose. I fear that you might not believe me and I fear the consequences.

First, I suppose, it would be prudent if not crucial to consider the source of the information that caused my madness; for the horror was not my creation. That distinction belongs to a man the gear world knows as Gearkegaard. How to describe this enigmatic figure? He is an impossible man. By that I do not mean that he is difficult, quite the opposite. He is impossible in the sense that you wouldn't think his existence possible. He is an implausible man. I am not being concrete, I know. Gearkegaard, not his real name, is the world's foremost expert on gears and gear design. He was one of my employees. He was already ancient when I arrived and in all the time I knew him he remarkably refused to age. He is one of those perpetually old men of indeterminate years. He is freakishly small but one often fails to notice. He is a man of science and technology who speaks little. His koan-like sentences carry overtones of philosophy or spirituality. He is an oddly interesting man, affable yet reserved, beneficent. I do not know how else to describe him. Imagine the intersection of science and theology taking human form and that is Gearkegaard.

I wonder how old Gearkegaard is faring in the new regime. He always appeared unflappable. Perhaps he is unaware that I am no longer there. I imagine him working away oblivious to the tribulations that most of us dwell on too often for too long. If he noted my departure it was probably with a shrug. Doctor, I am suddenly struck by the possibility, the probability even, that Gearkegaard—the unlikely deliverer of my insanity—may have disclosed his secret to my replacement. There is nothing to prevent him. Poor soul. What if another has been made mad? What if I am merely the first? What if it spreads like a virus?

I feel that I am getting ahead of myself as we get closer. Perhaps it is because we are getting closer, like a river approaching the falls. I am getting carried away. It was most likely my defective reaction to the news not the news itself that drove me insane. I fear a repeat of that reaction. I feel my emotions surge as we near the cause. No, I must slow down. I must breathe. Stay detached. Logic is the bulwark against anarchy. That sounds like something Gearkegaard would say. Gearkegaard is the source. And what he told me, what he revealed, made me sick and crazy and turned me into this sad comic figure sitting before you: an aging man locked away in a mental hospital searching for sanity.

RACK & PINION

Only through harmony can there be meaning in chaos, said Larry Chi Lun.

A compromise between right and wrong is always wrong, answered Grant Icahn.

Years before the Ear first heard the voice of God, back when Sobs played with Barbie dolls and dreamt of princes, Larry Chi Lun and Grant Icahn sat opposite each other listening to their bosses bicker. At the time, Larry Chi Lun was a support engineer for the California defense contractor Raygon, and Grant Icahn was a new hire with the State Department. The overcrowded debrief/outreach summit had been convened after the noisome Chang Affair. This forgettable meeting took place around an enormous oval table in a small room on the West Coast. Neither man spoke.

Gao Chang, a top Raygon engineer and Chinese

national, had been brought in for questioning by the FBI and accused of espionage. Chang, Chi Lun's uber-boss, friend and mentor, was—after a time, after the top-secret ink had dried and the inky political wrangling had been wrangled—formally charged with supplying classified documents related to aeronautical guidance systems to the Chinese government, the PRC. The Chinese immediately declared that they had nothing to do with this man, and that the accusations made by the US side were groundless. US officials were adamant that important classified information had passed hands and Chang was responsible. Neither side wavered. The problem with the Americans' position was that there was no real evidence against Chang. Proof and belief, however, run at different speeds and Chang was indicted. The case became a media circus. Day after day, strand by strand, the government's case unraveled. Eventually the accused was exonerated in the court of public opinion. All charges were then dropped and public apologies were made. Chang repatriated. The media moved on to the next scandal. Slightly embarrassed, the administration engaged in cosmetic damage control. The meeting at the enormous oval table in the small room on the West Coast was the government's answer to charges of racial profiling and cultural insensitivity in the badly botched case. According to official records, Larry Chi Lun and Grant Icahn had been face to face at that table in California. Neither remembered their first meeting. They would remember their second.

Larry Chi Lun was a spy. He was a deep cover Chinese operative. In fact, he was the person who had passed the classified documents cited in the Chang Affair to the PRC. Yes, he was a spy. Of that there was no doubt. Yet, revealingly, he never considered himself a real spy. Not really. Perhaps an agent, an asset maybe, but not a true spy, he told himself. He had never owned a gun, never poisoned anyone, never wore a disguise, didn't bribe, threaten or seduce. He considered himself a normal white-collar working man. He was an engineer and a considerate human being. He was a naturalized US citizen with a wife named Peggy and two children who wore blue jeans. He was a family man. A true blue American. Certainly he knew he was spying. When the PRC asked him to do something he did it, no questions asked. He felt it was his duty. It was part of who he was, but only a very small part, like an intermittent hobby. Anyway, he figured spying was part of the human condition. People spy on each other every day. It is a natural function. It is a normal part of life, integral. Everyone does it. Every day. It is all a matter of degree and perspective. And I spy for better reasons than most, all in the general pursuit of peace and fellowship, he told himself. Building a safer, better world through sharing.

Grant Icahn was a spy too, but a very different kind of spy than Larry. (Perhaps all spies think they're different from the rest.) Grant was a professional spy. It was his career. And he loved the spy game. He owned a gun, several in fact. He knew about poisons and disguises, drop sites and enhanced interrogation techniques. And he trusted only two things in this world: himself and American righteousness. He was a spy when he was with the State Department, he was a spy when he was with the CIA, and he was a spy as special assistant to Senator Overton Archer, the senior senator and living institution from the great and prismatic state of Texas.

Surely Senator—

Senator Archer held up his long-fingered hand and waited for his chief of staff and the others to leave his office.

Now, he said.

Grant continued.

Surely, Senator, you don't believe a word of that crap, do you? Tell me that you're not going to let them get away with this?

Easy there. Nobody's getting away with anything, Grant. Take a seat.

Grant, as ordered, sat down in one of the two straight-back leather upholstered chairs placed in front of the senator's bare oak desk.

You see the world as right and wrong, as black and white. And that's okay. It makes you good at your job. I'll let you in on a little secret. So do I, he whispered. But politics is another animal entirely. Politics isn't the real world. There's no right and wrong in politics. There just isn't. Trust me, I've looked.

Grant adjusted himself in his chair.

No, politics is about appearances. The eggheads call it optics now. Politics is about positioning. A successful politician has no enemies. He may have antagonistic friendships, but not enemies. A good politician is one who can smile while he's being stabbed in the back. That's politics.

But the issue here, sir—

I know the issues, Grant. I know what you know. I know 'Pathway to Citizenship' is a euphemism for amnesty. Everybody knows that. I know that the man who a minute ago was sitting where you are now was lying to my face. Everybody in the room knew it too. And he knew that I knew. But we all smiled, didn't we? We all played nice. That's politics.

Senator Archer rose from his chair and looked through the frosted panes of the white latticed window.

It's a rare occasion when you have to confront someone or something head on. Most times, if it comes to that you've already lost. This is not one of those times. This is a blip, Grant. A bothersome blip, perhaps, but a blip nonetheless. Those folks, those activists, those *voters*, get to walk away happy to have had some face-time with their senator. They get to go back to Texas and preach to their supporters that I was engaged and sensitive, that I understand the issues and their importance. They look good and I look good. But nothing happened, did it? Nothing was accomplished, nothing was achieved. We met. We shook hands. We talked. That's all. And that, Grant, that is politics.

Then, why the reconnaissance? Why prepare dossiers on them? Why go to all that trouble when you're just smiling and shaking hands?

We need to know who we're dealing with, said the senator turning to face Grant. I had to have something on them in the unlikely event they tried to become something other than blips. They are constituents. Like it or not they are my problem. The more you know about your problems the easier they are to eliminate.

Grant thought he perceived an opening.

These problems, these people, they are not going to go away just because you had a meeting. Securing our borders affects us all. And Texas is on the frontline. It's a matter of national security. The future of our country. Founding principles. The rule of law.

Now, I know you aren't questioning my patriotism, Grant. But let me remind you that there is no law against saying one thing and believing another. For the record, for you, let me state here and now that I will never support citizenship for illegal aliens, okay. Are we all clear on that?

Grant nodded.

And let me remind you about appearances. That old saw about them being deceiving is old for a reason.

Grant nodded again. The senator turned back to the window.

Did I ever tell you about the spitting fish of Polynesia? he asked. No matter, I'll tell you again. There are these incredible little fish called archerfish. Yeah, namesakes, I know. And they've got a special talent. These tropical little guys shoot drops of water to bring down their prey. They're aquatic snipers. By squeezing their gills together they can spit hard enough to knock bugs into the water where they're then gobbled up. Amazing creatures. Really amazing. Recently scientists studying them with these high speed cameras learned that archerfish actually adjust their little water jets to arrive with maximum impact over a range of distances. Extraordinary. They focus a fat liquid blob to gather just in front of the target, wherever it is. Apparently they do this by varying mouth opening diameter. What you get is dynamic jet control . . . from fish. Always hit their target. Always hit it with maximum force. And they do this, mind you, despite the optical distortion created by the water's surface. Wonderful creatures.

Grant turned to make sure no one else was in the room. He was never quite sure what the senator's animal stories were supposed to mean.

I expect that we could learn many a political lesson from our fishy friends and from the animal world in general, Grant. Don't forget that.

Grant said that he would be unable to forget it and he stood to leave. The senator kept talking to the window as Grant backed out of the room.

First, take your time to get it right. Consider all the angles. And, if you attack to kill, you better be damn sure to hit your target with everything you've got. I should get a few of those fish, an aquarium. It'd be a great conversation piece. Plus . . . .

On the other side of the country, where the blazing sun sets, Larry Chi Lun was also thinking about water. There wasn't enough. California was in its eighth straight year of severe drought. It had become a problem. And, as head of the Laurel Neighbors Association, it had become *his* problem.

What are we supposed to do?

You can't have it both ways.

I don't care. Pick one, for God's sake.

Tell me, how do I get around this?

Damned if I do, damned if I don't.

Every day he heard this or worse. People, his neighbors, his friends, were upset. Understandably, Larry told himself. He wasn't happy about it either. But this is a first world problem, he thought. No one was going without showers or drinking water. At least not yet. This was a problem of convenience, a problem of communication, a problem that, most likely, had a local solution.

The problem was this: Because of the drought California counties had imposed strict water usage regulations which prohibited the use of municipal water for the purpose of lawn maintenance. When grass does not get water it turns brown. The Laurel Neighbors Association charter demanded that ALL residences maintain uniformly green, weed-free lawns.

As president, Larry was required to fine property owners who break association rules. The brown lawn warning letters had gone out last week.

How do I keep my lawn green if I can't water it?

Are you going to pay my fine if the county catches me watering my grass?

Yours is brown too. Did you send yourself a letter, Larry?

Larry was caught between a rule and a dry place. Even his wife thought the situation had gone too far.

Can't you make an exception? Suspend the rule or something?

But Larry believed that rules were necessary to

maintain lasting order. Harmony rests on dependable impartial regulations, he reassured himself. He also believed that most problems had at least one solution. He was an engineer after all. He'd find a fix.

The first step was to buy time. He reread the association charter and discovered that there was no stipulated timetable for issuing fines related to lawn maintenance. He sent out a second round of letters explaining that fines would be put on hold—indefinitely—pending a more acceptable resolution. The pressure was off.

The second step was trickier. How could he resolve the opposing legal demands? How could he keep the grass green without contravening the county's edict? He sketched miniature irrigation systems that could reuse shower and tap water. He designed recirculating rainwater traps. He even consulted attorneys on the *force majeure* clause in the association charter. And then, one night watching the evening news as Peggy painted her fingernails, it came to him. Why couldn't he just paint the grass green?

For the next two weeks he practically lived in the garage. Peggy brought him sliced sandwiches and lemonade and told him he was working too hard. Larry fell into bed late at night and slept soundly. One Saturday morning he emerged from the garage riding a converted lawnmower. He had designed and built his own lawn-sprayer, a system devised to paint the grass. He called to Peggy.

It'll make the grass green, he said. And, to prove his point, he started the contraption and painted his fawn lawn a vibrant green.

Larry called a special session of the Laurel Neighbors Association to announce that he had come up with a solution to their watering problem. He introduced his machine, told them how to use it and declared that it belonged to their association.

Now anyone can have grass as green as they want.

Synthetically the neighborhood sprang back to life, emerald slivers reappeared between roads and roofs. Problem solved. Homeowners happy. And nobody dared utter a word about the faint, but persistent, chemical smell.

A few weeks later a local television station aired a story on the painted lawns and referred to the President of the Laurel Neighbors Association as Larry Chi Lawn. Larry and Peggy shared a good laugh.

The night grew a little darker and rivulets ran down the windows as the Ear prepared himself for bed. He wasn't thinking about spitting fish or green lawns—he had a Jesus fish affixed to the Lexus and a gardener named Carlos for his broad lawn—no, the Ear was thinking about Gearkegaard and his Monday morning meeting.

You look worried, said Mrs. Ear.

Work, that's all. Nothing life or death, he replied.

This too shall pass.

Stripes. Blue and white. Greece's colors, Magda would have noted. Wearing striped pajamas, the Ear squeezed striped toothpaste onto his striped toothbrush and began brushing his big, bright teeth.

Perfect, he thought, snarling rabidly into the mirror. Two front teeth shifted slightly at his tongue's touch. Maybe not so perfect, he reconsidered.

Sweetheart, would you make an appointment with Dr. Fremont? I think I need an adjustment.

His wife and his dentist were the only people in the world who knew that his captivating smile, a smile that had opened doors, a smile that set him apart, was principally a talented dental surgeon's creation, the ultimately positive result of a reckless accident. The Ear's smile was artificial. He spit and rinsed and spit again. Then he smiled for the mirror.

I'm in a difficult position, honey, said the Ear. It's that Gearkegaard person. He's not making it easy. It's a tricky situation.

I'm sure it will all be fine.

On the one hand I think he's necessary, but on the other he's destroying everything I'm trying to do. He's at the heart of the whole thing.

You'll find a solution. You always do.

I hope you are right.

Whatever will happen, will happen. After all, in the end, it's the Lord's will, not ours, she said. He knows best.

Evening ablutions complete, night-gowned and weary, they knelt down, closed their eyes, clapped their hands together and recited silent prayers. Finishing together, they exchanged quick pecks on the cheek and climbed into the large, firm bed. The Ear extinguished the lights. Outside, the rain fell.

SUN & PLANETS

Monday morning had never been busier. Everyone it seemed was at their desk early. And yet not a soul was working. They had all heard about the mandatory meeting between the Ear and Gearkegaard and nobody wanted to miss the presumed faceoff. Offices and cubicles were abuzz. Sam Binder was taking bets on the outcome. Half the staff wagered Gearkegaard wouldn't show. One or two newer hires even questioned whether Gearkegaard was a real person. Whatever they thought they kept mostly to themselves as they circled the hallways waiting and watching and wondering.

The Ear had arrived early too. He sat alone in his office asking God—well, the Lord, Jesus Christ, in sooth—to help him deliver the right words at the right time. It was two minutes before nine o'clock.

Good morning, Gwen. My dear, your beauty makes me forget I'm old. You are a shapely fountain of youth.

A resplendent smile eclipsed Gwen's flattered face as Gearkegaard continued.

We will talk about your exceptional beauty later, though. I've a meeting with the big man himself. The *new* big man. Must not be late.

For a short old man he moved apace. He was with Magda before Gwen's smile had time to transit her triangular face.

Nine sharp. And here I am. It's rather unlucky to be early, don't you think? It's like challenging fate.

Magda phoned the Ear to let him know that Gearkegaard—Lars—had arrived.

You may go right in.

The Ear had spent many weekend minutes anticipating this pivotal moment. Much would be determined by his opening remarks, by his comportment, his tenor. He had decided to be gracious. He had decided to meet his opponent more than half-way, hand extended, in an enthusiastic gesture of amity and collegiality. It did not go as planned. For when Gearkegaard crossed the threshold, the Ear's overeager right hand flew forward striking a sharp blow to the midpoint of his diminutive guest's forehead. Both men reeled, briefly. An inauspicious beginning. Acknowledging the faux pas, they each laughed self-consciously before shaking hands in a more conventional manner.

Although the Ear was silently rebuking himself for the blunder, Gearkegaard's height (or lack thereof) tended to catch most people by surprise, even those who knew him well. It was as if his dwarfism somehow disappeared in the amiable luminescence of his presence. In person he was a giant. Objectively, he was an elfin Santa Claus: a pudgy four and a half feet capped by a bulbous head framed in snowy white hair and little round spectacles.

Lars, I'm sorry, said the Ear. An unfortunate, but not insuperable, start, he thought.

While the Ear was apologizing to Gearkegaard for the miscalculated handshake, Blair and Corey were gossiping with Sam and Sobs about the closed door conversation.

I heard he's going to fire Gearkegaard. That's cold, said Corey. He looked at Sobs.

Don't be idiotic. The man is a living breathing institution. AGE will shut down before they'd let him go, answered Sam.

I wouldn't be so certain, Sam, said Blair. Our new CEO has his own way. He knows what he wants. He's not like that flake Lawrence. Please don't take that the wrong way, Ms. Sobchak. She acknowledged Sobs with a squint. No, our new chief knows how he wants things done. We'd be best served by following his lead.

The Ear's way or the highway, added Corey.

Sobs grimaced. Sam waved a hand.

You're all making way too much of this. He's a kid, wet behind the . . . well, you know, said Sam. He's just beating his chest, showing us that he's in charge. But he has no clue what he's doing. I can see it. He's in over his head. Things'll settle down after a time and he'll come begging for our help. Trust me. His directives, the great plan, this is all new kid on the block bluster. It's too heavy-handed to be real. It can't last. He'll ease up. He'll have to.

I wouldn't bet on it, Sam. But it looks like you already have, said Blair. To each his own, as they say. It's your funeral.

You take care of your business, Blair. I'll take care of mine. And, sure as I'm a man fit for pants, Gearkegaard will have no trouble taking care of his.

Look at those two, whispered Corey to Sobs. Quite a lot of friction between them, don't you think?

Not my concern.

You know friction can be a good thing. It makes things hotter.

Sobs rolled her eyes.

Soon your beloved Gearkegaard may not have any business to take care of, said Blair. Corey, come. We'll let these two get back to whatever it is that they do.

Corey vaulted himself from the corner of Sobs's desk and gave her a wink. Sobs pretended not to notice.

That woman could drive a man to drink. Well, what about it? Sam asked no one in particular.

On his way to the Ear's office, where he worried his boss was being terminated, Tom saw Corey rise from Sob's desk and give her a knowing wink. Tom sighed and hurried past.

Lars, I'm very sorry, said the Ear. That was not the way I wanted this meeting to begin. Please accept my apologies.

Gearkegaard nodded.

Now, on to business. Okay? Okay.

The Ear did the talking. After all, it was his meeting. Gearkegaard listened and passed the time stroking his short white beard like he was slowly working a snow cone.

For varied reasons and circumstances, I believe, we've gotten off on the wrong foot, as it were. We are out of sync. We are not in unison. The first reason for this get-together is to take a step back so we can march as one.

The Ear was happy with his extended metaphor. His wife, humming "Onward Christian Soldiers" on Sunday afternoon, had inspired the image.

As I don't have to tell you, working as one, working in tandem, side by side, hand in hand, shoulder to shoulder, cheek by jowl, is as important in management as it is in gears. Am I right? Yes, I can see we are in agreement. Frankly, Lars, this has not been happening. We have not been one. We have not been a team. And, I fear, you are *partially* at fault here. The Ear took a breath hoping that Gearkegaard focused on the partially part. Of course, I must accept some of the blame as well. The buck stops here, after all. Nobody's perfect. To err is human. Right? No reason to continue beating the horse. The bottom line is that we've both made mistakes. Haven't we?

A man who is without mistakes has not lived. And I have lived a long time, answered Gearkegaard.

Ha, yes, and so have I. But the past is past. And we cannot change our past. We can, however, prepare for the future. And preparation requires planning; it requires discipline. Now I understand that my methods are appreciably different than the previous administration's. Change is difficult. No one knows this better than I do. But our vision of the future needs to be a shared vision. I need to know that every single person on my team is following the same game plan, working from the same blueprint, reading from the same script. I need to know that I can trust you to follow my direction. I need to know that I can depend on you. I need to know if you are part of the problem or part of the solution.

The Ear stopped speaking and waited for an answer to a question that hadn't really been asked. Gearkegaard wasn't confident he knew what the Ear was talking about, so he waited a minute or two before he spoke.

I love what I do and I can't imagine not doing it, if that's what you're asking.

Good. Good. It's on record. *Nota bene*, said the Ear smiling. Done and done. Now we can move on to the second reason for our meeting.

On the other side of the door, Magda was telling Corey that for the past few days she'd had a strange premonition.

A strange furry feeling. It's the Evil Eye, she said. Someone's thinking ill of me. But why? I must ask my mother. She knows about such things. She is very knowledgeable. She has ways to make them stop.

Your mother? Is she a—

Tom was about to say witch, but Magda's earnestness made him mute.

My mother is a saint. Ninety-seven years old and has never been sick a day, answered Magda crossing herself and spitting quickly before burnishing the blue amulet around her neck. I would call her right now, but it is too early back home. She will probably call me first. She will sense that I need to speak with her. She knows these things.

Magda felt unburdened after talking about her furry feeling. Tom's discomfort was torqued up when he saw Blair and Corey approaching.

We're here for our nine thirty, Magda, said Blair. I know we're early birds. Does that entitle us to the worm?

Worms are magic. They should not be eaten. Not as powerful as bat bones, though. They can reveal the future and protect one from harm. And he is still with his nine o'clock, answered Magda. Please take a seat. I'll let him know that you are here.

Tom picked up an outdated copy of *Gears for Good* and kept his eyes down.

Pretending to read? Is it that bleak? Are you that worried your man is in there getting canned? asked Corey.

Nobody's getting let go.

Don't count on it.

What are you doing here anyway? asked Tom.

Hello!? The Hill trip is next week. Strategizing with the big dogs before the show. And you? Is it your job to haul away the corpse?

They're just talking. That's all. Talking. Like you and Sobs were.

Saw that, did you? I'm trying. She's a strange one. But get her out of those funeral clothes and I'll bet she's an animal.

68

She's nice, said Tom.

The princess of pessimism? Yeah, she's a regular bowl of sunshine.

The Ear excused himself to phone Magda and tell her that he was running behind and to please have Blair and Corey wait. He disliked letting his schedule slip. He felt it conveyed poor time management.

Sorry. I want to make sure we have enough time to discuss the second item on the agenda. We don't want bothersome interruptions, said the Ear. This is too important.

The Ear walked around his big desk and sat down conspiratorially in the semi-circular chair beside Gearkegaard.

This is where the rubber meets the road, Lars. Down to brass tacks and all that, he began. Gear design has stagnated. Oh, I don't mean that we haven't developed wonderful designs using the latest available technologies and materials. We have. You have. You've been doing a wonderful job. What I mean is that current gear design, in general, has become too specialized. It has become uninspired.

Engineering is only the application of reason to the world. We, as humans, are only partly reasonable, said Gearkegaard.

Precisely. Precisely. On one level that works just fine. It keeps things moving. Our customers are happy and that is vital. But in the bigger picture, in the grander scheme of things, we can't see the forest for the trees. We no longer entertain the big ideas. There's nothing new under the sun. Now, I know I don't have to tell you, but the last truly revolutionary breakthrough in gear design was in 1957. More than fifty years ago! Right, it was the harmonic drive—yes, I have read that you were involved in its creation. Space travel would have been impossible without it. Musser got all the credit. That was a big idea. It transformed the aerospace industry, didn't it? It changed the course of history. Well, I have it on very good authority that now is the right time for another big idea. We have waited long enough. I—and others—believe the time has come for the next transformative leap forward, the great gear after, the *ultimate* gear design. I call it the Great Gear. It will be the last gear design anyone will ever need. It will never wear down. It will be silent. It will be scalable, from microscopic to gargantuan. It will be perfect. It will, literally and metaphorically, move mountains. Imagine the applications. It will be last word in gear design. I believe it exists. I believe it's there for the taking. I believe it's within our grasp. And I have confidence that you, Lars Kilgore, will be the one to pluck it from the tree of knowledge.

I had a similar idea for many, many years, said Gearkegaard. And—

I knew it. I knew it. I should never have doubted the message. But to doubt is human, isn't it? To err, to doubt, we are but weak creatures. I struggle with my faith at times. Who doesn't? My trust must be absolute. Oh, Lars, I believe in the Great Gear. And I need you to believe in it too.

Gearkegaard said nothing but unhanded his beard. The Ear flashed a perfect, toothy smile and finished his evangelical patter.

All that we do here at AGE, the conferences, the consulting, the lobbying, it's all so pedestrian, so ordinary. It's necessary, it's valuable, but it's ordinary. And now by His grace we have been given something extraordinary. We have a higher purpose. We have been given a commandment of sorts. Nothing has a higher priority. I've cleared your plate—all those TBDs in our planning bible—so that you'd have the time and the resources to work our miracle. Whatever else you need, you just let me know. I'm here to help. Keep me updated.

I will.

I know you will.

When the door opened the Ear had his hand on Gearkegaard's shoulder. It was obvious he was anything but fired. Blair rose quickly and made her way to them both.

Lars, she acknowledged.

Blair, he responded. Good luck on the Hill.

The Ear broke up their icy glare.

Okay, Blair, now how are we going to wow'em in Washington?

Corey slithered behind Blair as the door started to close.

Relieved, Tom whispered to Gearkegaard.

How'd it go? Are you—are we—in some kind of trouble? What'd he say?

Gearkegaard placed his hand on Tom's shoulder. It barely reached.

A man who loves the sound of his voice will say anything, Gearkegaard replied.

The two men—one very short, one not short at all—waved 'see you later' to Magda. She smiled and thought to herself what a shame it was that two such nice men weren't Greek.

There is work to do, said the short one.

BACKLASH

Yes, Gearkegaard delivered the fateful message but I believed it and that belief gave it its awful power. Yes, we have arrived. I have arrived. I am prepared—as prepared as a permanently damaged man can ever be—to divulge what lies behind my break from reality.

I see no need for dramatics or specialized language, we are far beyond both. The simple fact of the matter is that one day Gearkegaard walked into my office and revealed to me that he had discovered, invented, created, designed—I suppose each word has its particular merits, its own bit of truth—the *perfect* gear assembly. I was face to face with mechanized perfection. To use yet another outdated term: the news blew my mind. And that is it.

You are disappointed. I can read it in your face. You were expecting more. You are disappointed and worried, worried no doubt that I might be more insane than you had previously concluded. Your worry, however, is unfounded. Perhaps my effort at clarity was too straightforward and too factual. But surely such a revelation requires no embellishment. I repeat, the man announced he was in possession of the *perfect* gear. I have emphasized the key word a second time for your benefit. And yet you do not react. It seems that I must do so once again. It was *perfect*. His discovery was not some ingenious improvement upon current gear technology. This was not some ordinary engineering advance. It was a machine—for in the end that's what gears are, simple machines—that was perfect. There's that word again.

You still look as though you do not understand. I sympathize. I had a similar reaction. At first I, too, did not believe.

Allow me to explain. Gears are amazing tools but they all have inherent problems because of their mechanical nature and use. Gears can slip when changing direction, friction causes wear, proper lubrication is a constant concern, teeth break, the mesh can be poor, and on and on and on. In addition, different types of gear assemblies perform different tasks, big and small, fine and massive, thus the indispensable role of a gear designer. Gears are built for a reason. What Gearkegaard had done—and God only knows how he did it—changes this forever. His perfect gear circumvents these issues. It would never falter. It would never break down. It would never fail. His perfect gear is scalable; it can be made to fit any purpose. Its use creates no vibration; it emits no sound. The implications are imponderable. Now do you understand what I mean by perfect? This goes way beyond mere technological innovation. This is a metaphysical breakthrough. This is an object that in our world is not supposed to exist. *Perfection* cannot exist. It is absurd.

And there you have it, a preposterous tale but one true nevertheless. Of course you must draw your own conclusions. You must decide what it means. On a more pressing note I am relieved to report my verbalization of the truth has had no immediate deleterious effect on my mental health. I am reassured. The medicine carries the day. I feel confident enough to proceed. I feel good, light. And I appreciate that you must have many questions, many of which I have asked myself and some of which we both know have no answer. Before we continue let me assure you for a final time that this was an actual event with actual ramifications. This *preceded* my illness. Furthermore, you misunderstand Gearkegaard if you harbor suspicions of impropriety. He is a mystical being. He has no ulterior motives. He acted as if he had developed the machine for his own private amusement. He didn't even have a name for it. I was told out of professional courtesy. Granted he was pleased by his invention, but he appeared more intrigued than anything else. He, too, was—although he did not say as much—curious about its future. Above all he had been fascinated by the word perfection more than by any other but he had perhaps fallen prey to the word. If there was any hint of pride it was there. This is gear perfection, he had announced. It was at that point I began my protracted contemplation of his discovery and its consequences.

I told myself, you must decide, whatever the cost. That was *my* dilemma. I became consumed by my deliberations which, as we now know, would eventually lead to my decline, my untimely rupture and my placement here.

Yes, I quite agree. The win-win trigger—jejune business jargon, indeed—prompted the destabilizing insight that the ideal cannot exist without horrific incomprehensible consequences. And that realization broke me. My neglected and diseased mind could not or would not imagine the possible existence of tangible perfection. It was too terrible a thought. It did not make sense.

The short answer is yes, I believed him. As I say this I recall reading somewhere that belief is the *civilized* form of innate and necessary deception. Belief is, by definition, deception. That being said, I saw the plans. I am an expert in the engineering field. This was no self-aggrandizing boast. Gearkegaard may be a magician but this was no trick. The gear was—is— real . . . as real as you or me.

What did Gearkegaard believe? Superb question. I don't know the answer. In general gear designers are a skeptical lot. They tend not to believe something works until they see it work. They have been taught that just because something looks good on paper does not mean it will work in actuality. But Gearkegaard is, if nothing else, unconventional. Years ago he told me that he didn't believe in anything. And I have never known the man to lie. If Gearkegaard lacks faith it's because he is in no need of it. He knows.

Are you familiar with Gaugin's masterpiece,

Where Do We Come From? What Are We? Where Are We Going? Of course you are. Who isn't? It is the definitive expressionistic work. The three scoops of primitive life, from birth to death, right to left, the vivid colors, the thick brushstrokes, the emotional, strength. It's majestic. Did you know that when Gaugin completed it he declared, *I shall never do anything better* and vowed to commit suicide? To this day there is great debate in the arts community whether he actually attempted to take his life but there is no question that he did not succeed. Yes, I have a two-fold reason for this brief deviation. First, Gaugin's painting epitomizes the eternal import of fundamental questions—like the idea of perfection with which I was confronted—and, second, when faced with such primal questions, what makes some go insane (Gaugin, me) whereas others (Gearkegaard, you) continue as if nothing had changed? As to the latter there must be a genetic component. There must be an adaptive benefit for one or the other. Faced with the inexplicable we either bend it to our will or are broken by it. We become saints or madmen. Perhaps there are yet unknown psychological limits to Homo sapiens. Perhaps some questions should not be asked. I have shown that this type of speculation is quite beyond me. I hope what I've revealed does not begin to haunt you. And, for the record, Gaugin was right. He never did anything better.

This either/or, saint or demon, aspect reminds me—and here I acknowledge that I am well off-topic—of my former stockbroker. It is not an elegant segue; it is free-association, I suppose. With your permission I will continue. Thank you. There is an expectation when you move up in the business world, that is, when you begin to make a certain amount of money, that you hire someone, a professional, to manage your assets. A large part of success in the corporate world is playing the game like everyone else so I hired a highly recommended broker to manage my money. He did not do a very good job. Very quickly I began to lose money. My broker sought to calm me by explaining that there were always temporary fluctuations in the market and that *we* were in it for the long haul. He asked me not to worry. He asked me to have faith. But I worried about losing my money. Concerned, I did some casual research and discovered that the stockbroker industry, financial services, asset management, or whatever they call it, which purports to be about numbers and trends and stochastic science, is actually, in the end, largely luck. I found that none of the listed, registered stockbrokers do a very good job for very long. Some are fortunate for a period, but sooner or later they all return to the mean, a very low mean, lower than the market average. Yet, as we know, like clockwork they each dutifully release detailed explications on why the past had happened the way it did and why the future will be as they predict. These explanations are then revised or forgotten. It is charlatanry, pure and simple. I took what remained of my money and invested it in an index fund and let it sit. Over the years I have beaten every *expert* on the Street. I say this not to brag. I do not know why I felt this important. It has something to do with confidence in being right or wrong, I suppose, or maybe it is about elements outside our control or understanding. I am not certain.

We have made progress, have we not? I feel that we have made progress. And this may also signify— may it not?—that I am well enough to go home. I do feel much improved, notwithstanding the nagging dyspepsia, this sour stomach, which most surely is a side effect of the tablets. I feel able to be on my own. I am not supposed to ask for my release, am I? Or maybe I am.

As a further sign that I am truly on the mend I would like to announce that I have made a friend within our clinical confines. Friend might be too strong a term. I have been caught in a lie. I have not had a friendship since my youth. Since I didn't have friends before I arrived it seems improbable that I would find one here. The only friends I have are the dead who have bequeathed their art to me, a fate less melancholy than it sounds. Doolittle, for that is what they call him, may not be a friend in the customary sense of the word but he has become more than an acquaintance, something of an ally as it were. And we can leave the definition there for the time being. I met Doolittle in all places at our group session. He joined me in quietly mocking the wallowing self-absorption so prevalent in the group. He is quite clever. He is also, of course, as mad as a hatter. He believes that he possesses the ability to communicate with animals. That's why they call him Doolittle, though I suspect that he rather likes the name and may have coined it himself. In addition it is clear that he suffers from severe OCD as his incessant blinking, constant repetitive movements and multitude of superstitions attest. Nevertheless I find conversing with him a welcome respite from the monotony of my incarceration. Yes, I jest, but about the incarceration not the pleasure of conversing with Doolittle. I understand that just because I am not free to leave does not mean that I am in prison. The joke was for your benefit. Doolittle would have gotten a chuckle out of it. He has a biting sense of humor and a chirpy laugh. You would like him. Yes, I know. He told me that he had a different doctor. He calls her *DSM* because he says that the manual is her entire world, it is her bible, and if something isn't in the *DSM* it doesn't exist. I find that droll. Most of the time he appears relatively normal, indeed one wonders what he did to get in here. Even when he talks about his— shall we say, unusual—abilities I find him compelling and believable. It is only later that one realizes the afternoon was spent listening to a middle-aged man recount his philosophical debate with a squirrel. He can be terribly convincing. The days pass more pleasantly with Doolittle. At a minimum he offers an intermission from my own thoughts. I presumed that you'd be pleased. Ah, you reveal your inner therapist when you say that pleasing you is not our purpose. I am sure we can agree that our purposes are manifold.

Doolittle's superstitions—oh, they are largely garden variety: avoiding ladders and cracks and the number thirteen, and so forth—evoke the habits of my factotum, my former executive assistant, Magda. There was no end to her silly Hellenic superstitions. It took me years to persuade her to stop littering the offices and hallways with sprinkles of salt. Don't ask me what it signified or allegedly prevented. I wonder how she is faring with the new CEO. She was near retirement. Perhaps she is already gone. And what about Blair? I'm sure she left for better prospects after not getting my desk. Sam will stay at AGE for life. Then again he would be just as content elsewhere. And all the others? Are they still there? Is gorgeous Gwen still greeting visitors at the door? Is she still answering the phones? Has she remarried? If she hasn't I'm sure she is well on her way. What is Rita writing about? She was able to make the most mundane event bubble with life. She should have been a novelist. Oh, and all the young people starting out: Tyler and Matt and Corey and Tom. Are they happy? Are they fulfilled? I was not a very good leader when I left. I had become, because of my illness, rude and dismissive. They most likely celebrated my departure. They are better off without me. Does Sid know about Gearkegaard's discovery? I wonder what he would make of it. He would attempt to disprove it—that is what he would do. Sid is, and always will be, a doubter. He is a born cynic. And what about my niece? What about Heather? She is on her own. I'm sure she feels that I abandoned her. Her mother probably told her as much. Yes, perhaps such relative musings are for another day. Yes, the pun was intentional that time. We shall explore family on another occasion.

My madness influenced many. I am not its only victim. And like the idea of the perfect gear itself, I will never fully understand, nor will anyone mortal, all its implications. Perhaps my illness was beneficial for some; perhaps they are better off without me; perhaps society is better off without me. And maybe—you may trust that I am not getting messianic—but maybe my breakdown caused Gearkegaard to abandon the project. He may have destroyed it. Maybe, in the end, my illness was for the good of humanity. You must admit the possibility exists. Maybe no one else—apart from you now—will ever have to consider the terror of realized perfection.

For weeks, doctor, weeks and weeks I tried to work out—and of course this was my first instinct— the consequences of Gearkegaard's perfect gear by means of logic and reason. I tabulated the pros and cons. I looked at the situation from every conceivable angle. But a solution, even a partial solution, was nowhere to be found. The search consumed me. It is the simplest thing in the world, I told myself, and I cannot understand why the simplest thing in the world eludes me. Perhaps I thought too much. I overworked the idea. I went back and scrutinized previous failed efforts. It became a case of superimposed logic perverting life. Perhaps there is no solution. Perhaps I depleted my dwindling mental resources on an intractable problem.

At one point the situation became so dire—my examinations having reached their nadir—that I made an attempt, an ultimately unsuccessful one, to discount Gearkegaard's revelation. I made a conscious effort to ignore the information he presented. I *pretended* that the gear did not exist. For a short time I managed to turn my back on the entire matter. I tried. But I didn't survive for long. You can't unhear or unsee something so profound. I kept working. I plodded along, continuing to function in a manner of speaking, my condition steadily worsening. I played my, by then, accustomed role issuing half-crazed orders to idiotic employees, before the lunacy—for that is what it was, a lunacy inspired not by the moon, but by an idea—gained the upper hand and took root. It was sheer and complete insanity. Sheer insanity—clinical madness, you call it psychotic depression—caused by an idea, one simple perfect idea.

I consider your question a provocation of sorts, doctor. But the short answer is, oh, yes. I believe it. I believe it with all my heart. I have to. Don't I? Don't you?

LANTERN

Matt marveled at the many marble monuments. White memorials sparkled in the morning sunlight. This was his first visit to the nation's capital and it showed. He waved at tourists. He looked to the sky for floating cherry blossoms. He didn't care. He poked his head through the taxicab's window to gain a better view. The wind roared. Rita sat next to him explaining how much the District had changed over the years. Matt didn't hear a word over the rush.

There was a time you could climb the Lincoln Memorial and no one would care. You could grab on to the wrought iron railing around the White House and try to see into the windows. These places, these statues, belonged to us all, no matter who you were. It was America's town. 'We the people' was more than just a phrase. Now it's security everywhere, barriers, you can't be here, you can't be there. Everyone is suspect. It's a quasi-police state. It's tense, nervous. It's ruined. It would, however, make for rather

84

captivating novel fodder, I imagine.

Look, the Washington Monument!

In the front seat Corey yawned.

It's huge!

The Ear and Blair shared a second taxi a few minutes and a few miles behind Matt, Rita and Corey. This was Blair's moment. This was her time to shine. This was her sweet spot. Lobbying was her life. It was what she was good at. And she was damn sure going to let the Ear know it.

Let's go over the schedule again. This afternoon we're with the House. We have a one o'clock with Shiner and Waxman, the party leaders of the Committee on Energy and Commerce. And then at two-thirty we have an assembly with the Commerce, Manufacturing and Trade subcommittee, every single member. That should be a scene. It's quite a coup to get them all in one room at the same time. It took a lot of work to pull it off, a hard soft sell.

Noted. I know how much you work, Blair. I know that you're good at what you do. You wouldn't be here otherwise, said the Ear.

Blair was deflated by the inadequate compliment. She tried a different tack.

We stick to our talking points at all times. That way we control the message. That's number one. Nothing is more important.

The Ear nodded while looking out the window.

Number two is to remember to whom you're speaking. The names and positions, where they're from, yes, that's one thing. But, more importantly, remember what they are about. Remember what motivates them. Congress is two very distinct entities, each with its own implicit paramount interest. House members are about reelection. Senators are about legacy.

That's rather cynical.

This is a cynical town, answered Blair. Remember that too.

Both taxis made for the same hotel from the same airport. Their drivers chose contrasting routes.

It's really a hill, screamed Matt. It really is. It's Capitol Hill. And this afternoon we're going to be under that big white dome. Incredible. Just incredible.

Corey turned around and yanked Matt back into the car.

Hey, hayseed, you want to tone it down a bit. First, we won't be in the Capitol. We'll be across the street in an office building. Second, this isn't a tour. You're not on a junior high school class trip. And, third, you're acting like such a bumpkin our cabbie may never get us to the hotel. I can see the out-of-towner dollar signs in his eyes.

Aren't you worried he'll hear you?

I doubt he speaks much English, said Corey.

Matt sat in silence for the rest of the journey. He reminded himself that he was a professional, that he was an adult. He was paid to be here, paid to be in Washington D.C. Quietly, he still couldn't believe it. When they arrived at the hotel the meter's red numbers read $32.50. The Ear's cab had arrived fifteen minutes earlier for a price of $18.75, which included tip. AGE corporate credit cards settled both fares.

Congressman Shiner's office was as impressive as the monuments, thought Matt. Starched flags on eagle-tipped poles flanked an imposing desk. Pictures of presidents, present and past, dotted the wood paneled walls. The chairs were plush and noiseless. Matt, Rita and Corey were assigned seats against the east wall, while Blair and the Ear gathered around Shiner's desk. Waxman sat next to Blair, closely.

After Blair made the introductions her role was over, unless, that is, the Ear got himself into trouble, unless he worked himself into a corner or hesitated too long in answering a question. He was the boss, the chief executive. And one never overshadows the boss. So, Blair crossed her legs looking pretty and professional, a pleasant distraction for the two long-time congressmen. She disliked this part of her job. She detested the temporary, but necessary, demotion to ornamentation.

The Ear performed well. His rehearsed speech sounded extemporaneous. He was affable. He stayed true to his talking points. He didn't digress. He fielded questions with deference and aplomb. Blair was surprised and relieved.

It was obvious to everyone in the room that Shiner and Waxman disliked each other. They competed. They were contrary. If one said black, the other said white. And, yet, they somehow still managed to say pretty much the same thing.

America moves on gears, I like that, so true, said Waxman.

Yet I trust we all share the opinion that *American* gears make America move better, said Shiner.

87

Job-creating manufacturers made this country great, said Waxman.

Industrial wage-earners built this country, said Shiner.

Americans can compete and win against anybody in the world.

In a global economy the playing field must be level. It must be fair.

Profit-driven research and development will keep us number one.

As a society we must invest in new technologies and new ways of doing business.

The brief, dichotomous meeting ended with all present enthusiastically agreeing that a dominant America is the best possible state of affairs for every American and the world's population in general.

At the ritual handshake-trading Rita escaped and returned with the congressional photographer. She posed and reposed the four principles over and over as the photographer clicked away until an aide reminded Shiner that he had another appointment. Rita had what she needed. She started to write the press release in her head.

Organized chaos, that's what Blair told them to expect from the Commerce, Manufacturing and Trade subcommittee. She was half right.

The room was congested and loud. Aides and staffers ran back and forth, slamming big wooden doors strategically placed at the center of the four long paneled partitions. Several lawmakers were already in the room barking out orders, their thumbs tapping on tiny phones.

Okay, here we go, said Blair. The five visitors from AGE fanned out. Blair and the Ear targeted the congressmen or congresswomen or congresspersons. The other three had been assigned specific sections of the capacious room and their task was to intercept and detain anyone who entered their section. They were to introduce themselves and then diplomatically attempt to seat them quickly in preparation for the Ear's big speech. Rita was a natural. She had no difficulties coaxing the over-worked public servants into the comfortable chairs. Corey hunted for comely female aides. Matt was consistently ignored. He had to physically seize the person to get noticed. After ten minutes of wrangling the room was quiet enough for Blair to thank everyone and introduce the Ear.

Esteemed lawmakers, colleagues, friends, it is my pleasure to present to you the chief executive officer of the American Gear Enterprise, Paul Briar.

The Ear delivered roughly the same speech he had given Shiner and Waxman. Blair thought it best to keep things simple. Again, he delivered it well. He stayed on point. It was a success.

Some lawmakers listened. Some did not. Almost all were engaged with their phones while the Ear spoke. Two left during the short speech. One was in Rita's section. She thanked the congresswoman from Michigan for attending and handed her an AGE folder. The other departure was in Matt's section. For a second or two Matt considered trying to stop the California representative from leaving. Instead he pretended not to notice.

When the speech ended the room emptied. No one asked any questions. No one seemed moved or disappointed. These were very busy people. A few instructed staff to remain. The representatives who stayed were either from manufacturing districts or they were Blair's friends. The meeting petered out to the sounds of hushed small talk.

That went outstandingly, said Corey packing up his belongings.

We captured some powerful images, said Rita. I thought both meetings went wonderfully. This was a hoot.

It's too early to know how much of our message got through, said Blair. Our follow-ups will tell the story. But, overall, I'd say that today was a win.

I don't know, Blair, said the Ear. I don't feel like we hit one out of the park.

This trip is not about scoring, she said. There's no pending legislation we're asking them to move on. When there's a bill we need, that's when we keep score. This trip is about not making mistakes. And we didn't. That's a win in the lobbying game.

Matt didn't think the 'game' went well at all. And a day that began so brightly with so much promise now seemed gray and dull. Perhaps he had unrealistic expectations. But it seemed to him that everyone was just going through the motions. It was pretense. The lawmakers were here in body only, he thought. Their attention was elsewhere. This could've been about anything: gears, immigration, climate change, religious freedom, nuclear weapons. It wouldn't have mattered. It was all for show. It was a show for the sake of a show. It was a waste of time. It felt like a sham. He started to think that the hallowed House halls were hollow. Humph, he huffed.

In any event, I thank you all, said the Ear. Now let's get back to the hotel, have something to eat and get a good night's rest. Tomorrow is another day.

Almost nothing was happening at AGE. With the Ear and Blair in Washington, the offices were quiet. Gearkegaard was offsite with Sid. And Sam had gone for a liquid lunch and never returned. The underlings were in charge. Gwen sat at her desk but the phone didn't ring. She worked on her never-quite-perfect, painted nails, played on the computer and waited for the clock to strike five. Magda sneezed twice and wondered who was talking about her and if it was one or two people. Tom was at Tyler's desk. They were playing *Words with Friends* on their phones. Tom had just played the word JOBS and was now ahead by thirty-eight points. Sobs sat at her desk listening to a podcast. Tom sneaked long peeks at her when it was Tyler's turn.

You get all the good letters, complained Tyler.

Sorry, said Tom.

Why don't you just go over there and talk to her. The leering is making *me* uncomfortable.

No, I don't want to bother her. She looks peaceful. I'd hate to mess that up.

Fine, remain celibate. It's your turn. And, by the way, all I have are vowels. Let me play at least.

Sobs was listening to a pair of psychologists discussing why people see Jesus's image in toast slices and tree bark. According to the experts we are all hard-wired for pareidolia—seeing faces and other recognizable images where they don't exist—but what we see is determined by personal expectations or beliefs. Buddhists see Buddha, Christians see Christ. This phenomenon is an offshoot of apophenia, which they defined as the perception of patterns or connections in random or meaningless data. The psychologists were debating whether this patternicity, as they called it, was a clinical problem, something to be treated. Seeing patterns and connections in random things? Sounds a lot like life, thought Sobs. Hasn't every human being who has ever been born on this blue dot located somewhere amid countless universes made connections in the chaos, discerned patterns in the darkness? Isn't that what we all do, every day, always? She looked out the window. It was an ordinary day. There was nothing to see.

You are too skilled, Tom. I resign. I surrender. I am defeated.

One more game?

I'm afraid not. I must be off. And the time has come to face your fears. Talk to her. Go on.

Maybe another time, said Tom.

Sobs! Hey, Sobs, Tyler yelled.

Sobs removed one earbud.

Your boy here knows too many words so I'm going shoe shopping. I shall not return. Hold down the fort. And you two play nice. *Au revoir.*

Tom hesitated. He wasn't sure if he should stay or go. He looked at her and hoped that she'd remove the other earbud. It would be a sign she wants me to stay, he thought. She didn't remove the plugged earbud. Nor did she replace its dangling twin. Is that a sign? He felt he was being ridiculous. He had to do something.

What are you listening to?

It was a beginning.

Day one with the representatives had been spent south of the Capitol. Day two was with senators. The Senate offices were clustered on the opposite side of the Capitol, north of the giant white cupola.

We're movin' on up, sang Rita.

Blair had the Ear scheduled to meet individually throughout the day with a dozen senators, all members of the important Commerce, Science and Transportation Committee. She had also hoped that a drop-by or two might result in additional contact. And there was always the chance they might run into an important staffer or senator in a hallway.

After introductions, the Ear made his speech. It was the same one he'd made to the House members with a word or phrase, here and there, altered to appeal to the nobler senatorial sensibilities. The meetings went predictably. There were many understanding smiles and nodding heads. Blair was satisfied. The Ear was not. He had hoped for more. He had hoped for votaries. Two senators had even cancelled at the last minute.

For Matt and Corey it was a long day made longer by tedious repetition. They sat. Then they moved to another office, another building, and sat some more. They carried folders, pamphlets and other paraphernalia and once or twice rushed to make emergency copies. But they didn't meet anyone. They barely spoke. They stared at carpet patterns. They did as they were told. They worked.

At the tail end of each meeting Rita charged in with the senate photographer to document the event.

The final scheduled meeting of the day was with Senator Overton Archer of Texas. Although he was a minor player on the Commerce Committee, he was the chairman of the Armed Services Committee, and, as such, was a towering figure in the Senate, on the Hill, and in the country. Secretly, Blair had been surprised when his office accepted the meeting request. She had never developed much of a relationship with his staff.

At first they thought Senator Archer was alone in the room. Then they saw Grant Icahn lurking in a far dark corner.

Don't mind him, said the senator, I think he lives here.

The senator introduced the man in the corner as his very special assistant and they all exchanged handshakes. Grant held Blair's hand a little too long. The Ear thought the senator's special assistant looked like a body guard. Blair thought he looked like a spy.

When he'd finished his well-practiced speech, the Ear was convinced he'd delivered a masterful performance. He had been clear, but passionate. The senator was not impressed.

I hear you there, Mr. Briar. America moves on American gears. That's good. And Lord knows we don't want to lose any more jobs to foreign countries.

He paused and clicked his tongue.

The other day I was reading a story about this amazing little insect. It's called Issus. It's a kind of planthopper. Well, apparently, when they're young, as nymphs, they have a gear-like mechanism on their legs that helps them jump. They lose it when they reach adulthood. Incredible, right? I thought you of all people would appreciate it. Now, there are two pertinent lessons here. The first is that apparently we aren't as clever as we thought. Nature had already developed gears long before we did. We're not so special. Are we? And the second and most instructive part, I think, is that this Issus fellow only needs its gear while it's young. After that it finds a better way of doing things. Why? Because gears breakdown after a time. And a breakdown would mean death to the little critter. Amazing, right? So maybe, just maybe, we'll find a better way of moving ourselves without the need for gears. Seems logical enough, doesn't it?

The Ear couldn't believe his ears. He turned a purplish-red.

Blair was about to step in when Grant told the senator that he had a hard stop in two minutes. The senator thanked them both kindly for the visit.

You're wrong, said the Ear.

Excuse me, said the senator.

He didn't mean that you were wrong, corrected Blair.

Yes, I did, said the Ear, firmly. You're wrong. You don't abandon man's greatest invention because of some insect.

I'm sorry, Senator—

But he's wrong, Blair. Senator, what if I told you that we are about to unveil the ultimate gear, the Great Gear, one that will transform how we do everything, from ballistics to business? It's a silent, scalable, secret weapon. It will never break down. And it's ours. What would you say to that?

If such a gear exists, I'm grateful that it's in your capable hands, said the senator. And now I am sorry, I really have to move on to my next appointment. Again, thank you for coming in.

Rita and the photographer entered. No one but the senator smiled. The Ear's perfect teeth stood behind pursed lips. Grant instinctively maneuvered out of frame.

Behind the closed door, Grant asked the senator if he thought such a gear could exist.

Life is strange. Who knows? To be on the safe side let's inform ET and C. Maybe they've heard something.

Right away, Senator.

And, Grant, why don't you stay close to those AGE people? See what you can find out about this super gear.

Outside, on Constitution Avenue, Blair asked the Ear if he had any idea what he had done.

What happened to staying on message? You don't tell the senior senator from Texas and the chairman of the Armed Services Committee that he's wrong. You don't bluff these people. You can't.

It was a Hail Mary, said the Ear. A Hail Mary.

The Wineskeller Bistro stood on a little square off DuPont Circle. Blair had chosen it for its reputation and its architecture. Upstairs was a large room where people could mix and mingle; downstairs was a maze of small shadowed alcoves, perfect for more private conversations. At dusk the group from AGE walked through the front door.

Blair told them that free drinks and free food was no guarantee of success.

You never know who'll show, she said. We're sure to get some aides and other staffers, but be on the lookout for the whales. We might even draw a cabinet member. You never know.

Everyone they'd met on the Hill had been given an invitation. In addition, select gear manufacturers from around the country had been flown in to hobnob with the Washington elite. It was to be a social affair for a hundred. Blair checked on the preparations. Matt and Corey ordered a beer. Rita read a draft press release to the Ear.

By ten o'clock the Wineskeller was full. Two senators had come and gone. Two representatives remained. One was beginning to get drunk. The senior staffers started to leave and around eleven the last two lawmakers poured themselves into a cab. Blair informed the Ear that the evening was over.

Some of these folks will stay until they're kicked out, she said. But they're little fish. There's nothing much left to do. The schmoozing is done. You can go back to the hotel now if you'd like.

The Ear disliked barrooms and couldn't wait to leave.

Thank you, Blair. It was a nice evening. Good turnout.

Rita rushed up to ask if she could share the Ear's cab. She wanted to get back to the hotel to work.

Rita's gotta write, she joked.

And Blair ordered another Tanqueray and tonic, her third.

And Corey flirted with a red-headed waitress in a dark alcove.

And Matt ordered his fifth beer from the old bartender and collapsed onto a stool.

Then, at eleven-thirty, Grant Icahn arrived.

Blair was unprepared for a late arrival, especially an influential late arrival. She slammed down the remainder of her drink and almost tripped running toward the door.

Grant, you made it, she slurred slightly. I'm afraid most everyone has left. Let me get you a drink.

Allow me, he said. And what will you have?

Grant carried his Dewar's on the rocks and her Tanqueray and tonic to the nearest nook where Blair waited, crossing and uncrossing her legs.

Was it a good party while it lasted? Did I miss anything? Don't tell me your boss punched out a Supreme Court justice?

Blair laughed.

No, it was quite boring actually. And my boss was very well behaved. She leaned in closer to Grant. He doesn't drink, you know. Sshh, it's a secret.

Blair took a long sip of her drink and Grant

observed that she was drunk. He thought she looked prettier like this, like the alcohol smoothed the rough edges, but maybe it was just the shadows.

Please tell Senator Archer that I am sorry. Tell him that I am, personally, very sorry.

No need, said Grant. He was amused. It takes more than that to ruffle the old bird's feathers.

Corey crept from his alcove. He was going to ask Blair if he could walk his waitress home. He saw Blair lean in toward Grant. He decided he didn't need her permission.

What are you guys in town for? asked the bartender, passing Matt another beer.

We're here to buy as much democracy as we can.

There's plenty for sale, that's for sure.

How can you live here? asked Matt. How can you take it? Everything's fake, everybody's for sale. It's a horrible, horrible place.

It has its good and bad, like anywhere, I suppose.

I don't know. I couldn't take it, said Matt. Don't know how you people do it.

Years ago, started the bartender, a group of gargantuan Nordic-looking guys were sitting at that table over there drinking and drinking. There were four or five of them, I think. And, man, were they loud. And they kept getting louder and louder the more they drank. The place was packed. We tried to get them to keep it down, but they had no idea what we were saying. They didn't speak a lick of English. Every time we tried to adjust their volume they'd offer to buy us drinks. We couldn't just kick them out for being loud. In this town you never know if somebody's important or not. So you've got to be careful, diplomatic. And today's nobody could be tomorrow's somebody. They could have been from one of the embassies. You never know. And plus we're trying to run a friendly business here. Well, they keep getting louder and it's starting to bother the other customers. The manager is asking me what we should do when one of our waitresses walks up to the guys and babbles something to them. Immediately the guys clam up. They get all embarrassed and quiet. Turns out the waitress speaks fluent Finnish. The girl couldn't make change without help and here she is speaking Finnish. And that's D.C. It's where power meets weird. You never know what'll happen next. How could you not like it?

I have no idea if the magic gear is real, said Blair. That was the first time I heard about it. I was—hiccup—as surprised as anybody.

It would be a pretty big deal if it were true, said Grant. The implications for UAVs alone would be staggering.

What are UAVs?

Unmanned airborne vehicles. Drones.

You're cute, said Blair. Are you a spy?

I do what my boss tells me to do. If that makes me a spy, then I'm a spy.

Me too, I guess. I've always toed the line. Always done the right thing. And look where it's gotten us. I mean me. I mean we should have another drink.

WORM

Larry Chi Lun was painting his lawn when he got the call. Peggy trotted out with a glass of pink lemonade in one hand and the silver cordless in the other. A monotone, male, Chinese voice told Larry that engineers at the American Gear Enterprise had created a superlative gear and it was his duty to obtain said wonder gear for the PRC. And that was it. The transmission ended.

The brief, blunt message did not scream espionage. It wasn't sent to some secret, untraceable burner phone. The Chi Lun's number was in the phone book. The man did not speak in code, unless Mandarin counts as code. The line was not secure. No precautions were taken. It was straightforward overt communication. It was all so simple, so clear. Larry got the message. But he had no idea how to proceed.

The Ear was in a similar pickle. He had told a lie, a

101

whopper. In a fit of amateurish fear he had twisted around and bitten his own tail—and in front of a US senator. He, too, needed the Great Gear. And he needed it now. And he had no idea how to proceed.

This must be part of the Lord's grand plan, he told himself. Jesus knows why I stretched the truth, why I let the gear out of the bag, so to speak. No harm done, I suppose. It's what I was meant to do. All part of His plan.

Out of the bag the Great Gear quickly became great news. No longer was it a susurrant secret between the Ear, Gearkegaard and Jesus of Nazareth. Blair, Grant and Senator Archer of Texas now knew about it. The Emerging Threats and Capabilities (ET and C) subcommittee knew about it. Matt and Corey, Rita and Gwen, Tyler, Sam and Magda knew about it. Sid knew about it. Larry Chi Lun and the Chinese government knew about it. Tom knew about it. Even Sobs knew about it.

Sobs knew about it, but she believed in the Great Gear like she believed in most things. She didn't. To be more exact, she didn't care. None of this matters, she said. Meaning is an illusion, a false construct, built to mollify the masses. She wasn't depressed. She wasn't sad. She was realistic. She was honest.

Nothing in her past predicted such pessimism. Sure, she never knew her father, but she was raised by a loving, self-sacrificing mother of modest, but sufficient, means. She never lacked for much. She had a medium-sized backyard and a dog named Arthur. There were more than a few people over the years who considered her a friend. Though she did her best to hide it, she possessed a dark physical beauty that had attracted a frustrated series of pimply suitors. She went on dates. She wasn't a recluse. This wasn't some extended hormonal teenage angst heightened by the Cure or the Smiths or Mahler. This wasn't a phase. This wasn't something to get through. This was life, pointless life. Hers was a bookish nihilism based on philosophy, science and history. Knowledge is not possible, she had concluded. She got good grades, even aced her SATs. She turned her back on higher education, however, and opted for a biweekly paycheck courtesy of Uncle Darryl and AGE. Throw myself into the maw of the rabble, she said, might as well get on with it. Existence was a trivial abyss. Yes, she had it figured out at a very young age. There were no mysteries to solve. No lessons to learn. Live, then die, and back to nothingness. So, no, she didn't care about gears, great or small. They didn't matter to her. In the scheme of things nothing mattered.

Oddly, cherubic Gearkegaard had reached the same lonely conclusion. Life was meaningless in the scheme of things, except there was no scheme. But this he discovered later, much later, in life. And that made all the difference in their contrasting attitudes.

Gearkegaard didn't really care about the Great Gear either. Rather, he didn't care about the idea of a great gear. He cared about the work. He cared about the engineering. He liked to fix things. He liked designing and creating. He liked doing.

Living long had made Gearkegaard a witness. He had seen people die. He had seen courageous, selfless acts. He had seen awful cruelty. He had seen kindness and he had seen love. Seeing these things, witnessing, changes a person. Experience reshapes. Of course, none of this mattered in the nonexistent scheme of things, but they mattered to him. And that was what mattered, he had decided.

Yes, there is no point to life. Agreed. But, then, what is the point to its opposite? Gearkegaard was a practical man. One either lived or one did not. Yes or no. He had concluded that life was worth living. He had his reasons. There may be no foundational answers in the big, but in the small maybe there's something to work with. Get your hands dirty and make yourself and others a little happier. It's a yes or no proposition, he'd told himself, life or not. And if the answer is yes then you do it right. You do it to the best of your abilities. A simple yes or no.

Sid was sarcastically laughing. It's ridiculous. Great Gear, my round brown Hindu ass, he said slapping his forehead.

Tom believed that if the Great Gear could be found Gearkegaard was the one to do it. The man was a magician. He was explaining the thorny art of gear design to Sobs. She was paying half attention while flipping through a nametag catalogue.

It's just puzzle pieces working together. That's all it is. Why shouldn't we be able to get them to work together perfectly or close enough?

Tom believed in the idea of a perfect gear. It made sense to him. It was logical. It was comforting.

What an amazing concept. Imagine, he said, it would change literally everything.

Nothing will change, said Sobs.

Tom didn't understand her blanket negativity. He thought it was an act or that she'd been hurt, badly. He believed in sympathy. He believed in cause and effect. Something had caused her to think this way. The corollary to this is that something else can cause her to change, to care. He wanted to be that something.

Tom came from a long line of cradle-to-grave Roman Catholics. He believed in the Trinity and the virgin birth. Yes, he had been an altar boy who sometimes fell asleep during Mass, but he was as Irish as overcooking the Sunday roast. He believed in family and in a loving God and, although the church didn't have all the answers, it had enough for him. He thought Sobs could use a few answers.

Come on, Tom. Let's go hear about this glorious gear, laughed Sid.

Tom waved bye to Sobs. She waved back.

Grant told the senator what Blair had said.

I think Briar's kept them in the dark. He's either crazy or he's sitting on it. The others didn't know about it. I believe that she's telling the truth.

A hungry dog believes in nothing but meat, said the senator.

Grant didn't understand how that applied, so he waited.

Why don't you take a trip out there and see what you can see. Dig around a bit.

I've been given worse assignments, thought Grant.

And how did the PRC hear about the Great Gear? That's a valid enough question. It's a truism that there are spies everywhere. It could have been a spy, a mole. It could have been an accident. It could have been any number of things. In the end, it doesn't much matter. And that's something in itself. There are times it doesn't matter how you know something, just that you know it.

Larry didn't ask himself how the PRC knew about the gear any more than he asked himself why they'd chosen him for the mission. That didn't matter. He asked himself how best to get to AGE. That was what mattered. That was the task at hand. Since his employer, Raygon, was a substantial dues-paying member of the American Gear Enterprise, it was not difficult. He picked up the telephone and dialed. Gwen forwarded the call to Magda.

Larry lied. He told Magda that next month he'd be in town on business and had hoped that someone there might have free time to talk. We engineers like to connect, he said. Magda was amenable. AGE staff had been trained (Directive # 17) to never say no to member requests.

Yes, we can arrange that. When would you like to visit?

Oh, um, any day the week of the fifth, bluffed Larry.

Perfect. He's onsite that week. I'll squeeze you in at your convenience.

How about Tuesday then?

Oh dear, said Magda. I am sorry. Anything but a Tuesday. Tuesdays are very, very unlucky. I hate to schedule anything on a Tuesday if I can help it.

Okay, how about Thursday, said Larry, that's the eighth. And eights are very, very lucky.

They are? Wonderful. The eighth it is. How's ten o'clock?

Excellent. I'll see you then. Oh, one more thing. Might I be able to meet with other staff while I'm there?

I don't see why not. I'll take you around myself. We'll give you the VIP tour. How's that?

Perfect. Thank you.

Blair, Washington on line two. A gentleman calling from Senator Archer's office. A Grant Icahn? Who's he? He sounds dreamy.

Thank you, Gwen. I'll take it from here.

Blair unconsciously fixed her hair.

Blair Hunt.

Grant Icahn. Remember me?

Of course. The spy. What can I do for you?

Formal. Okay. The direct approach then. I will be in your neighborhood next month and I thought it would be nice to see you. Maybe grab a drink.

No more drinks for me. I still have a headache from the last time. Will the senator be with you?

It would be an unofficial visit.

Why?

If I need a reason let's say it's to recover the tracking device I left in your bag.

Funny.

What about an alcohol-free lunch?

Okay.

Tuesday the sixth?

I'll clear my schedule.

Great, I'll pick you up at noon. I can't wait to see the American gear industry's mission control. It'll give me the opportunity to plant a few bugs, maybe a camera or two.

The Ear wasn't listening. He was imploring.

What can I do to speed things up? How can I help? I'm afraid our situation has changed. We need it right away. Yes, I realize that we hadn't discussed deadlines. And I understand this is exasperating news. You're vexed. You must be. But it must be done this way, do you understand? It's outside my control.

Is he for real?

Siddhartha, do you have something constructive to add? asked the Ear.

I just said . . . so this is real?

However much or however little Lars chooses to share is none of my concern, but I assure you that the Great Gear is very, very real.

Gearkegaard was silent. He did not contradict the Ear.

It's real, isn't it? Tom asked Gearkegaard.

It's impossible, this god gear, said Sid.

Don't be blasphemous.

Okay, supreme gear, whatever.

Supreme makes it sound like it comes from North Korea, said Tom.

How about—

Enough! It is great, said the Ear. It is the Great Gear.

Whatever you call it it is ridiculous, not to mention impossible. We are not sorcerers. This is not make-believe. We are materialists. We need specs. We need requirements, details. We are engineers. Tell him, boss.

Gears are designed for a purpose, not just to exist, said Gearkegaard.

The primary purpose of the Great Gear, said the Ear, is to exist. Applications will come later. That is not your affair. Your job is to bring it to life.

Bring it to life? It's a gear.

Gearkegaard shifted in his chair. Then he rose and confessed. The Ear was all ears.

On paper it already exists. As I said before, I had a similar idea long ago. Theoretically it is done. I completed it over a year ago. It was finished before you even mentioned it. But gears do not work on paper or on computer screens. They must work in the real world. They have to be constructed. They have to function. Then we'll know.

So build it, build two. I don't care. Just do it quickly.

We will do our best, said Gearkegaard.

That was what the Ear needed to hear. His big white teeth beamed.

Splendid. Let me know as soon as you have it then. And, gentlemen, allow me to remind you that we believe before we know.

The three engineers left the room in various states of disbelief.

You can't be serious, said Sid.

I do not tell lies and I do not do what I hate, said

Gearkegaard. In any case this is my burden. I must do it alone.

Sobs watched the three men hurry by. They were arranged by height with gnomish Gearkegaard leading the way. Tom was stuck in the middle. She was surprised by a sudden hope that Tom would look to her and wave. He did.

She returned the wave and daydreamed about their unlikely, unfolding friendship. She enjoyed being with him, she confessed. He was polite, respectful and adorably awkward. It was obvious that he liked her. It was cute. It was safe, harmless. And she liked herself more when she was with him. He made her feel that it was enough to be who she was, like he didn't need her to be something or someone she wasn't. He made her feel warm. He made her feel comfortable. Nothing wrong in a little comfort, now and then, she thought.

Later, Tom and Sid were briefing Corey about the Great Gear get-together.

Sounds like the old man has lost his mind, said Corey.

The Ear is a man with large teeth and small abilities, said Sid.

He sure can talk, though, said Tom.

Any idiot can talk.

Corey waited a suitable amount of time before addressing Tom.

Speaking of talk, what, I go away for a few days and you make a move on my girl?

What? Who?

Sobs, that's who. Don't give me that look. I know you've been making your move.

Your girl? I—

Don't sweat it, Romeo. I'm only kidding. Not my type anyway. Too blah. Now, that ginger waitress in Washington, you guys should've seen her. She was alive. She was colorful.

Tom, almost smiling, said nothing.

Ah, the worm turns, thought Corey. The worm turns.

FRICTION

I will confess to considerable ignorance when it comes to psychotherapy but I am surprised it has taken this long, that after so many hours in deep discussion only now are you inquiring about my upbringing and my family. I assumed, or so I previously assumed, that according to your profession the origins of most mental illnesses were routinely located in the early years of life. I was mistaken. Perhaps I had believed this because it is invariably perpetuated in this manner by the television and movie industries. Perhaps your field is more advanced than it is portrayed. No, I admit my thinking was faulty.

My parents were no different than thousands or even millions of others across the country. They were neither rich nor poor; they were neither smart nor stupid. They were not exceptional in any way that I can remember. They were normal, a product of their time. My father was a postal clerk and my mother was a homemaker. What a word! *Homemaker.* It is a relic. It belongs to another era. The moment the word left my lips I was possessed by a feeling of mortification, as if I had said something inappropriate and somehow offensive. It is astounding how rapidly language changes in one's own lifetime. Our middle to lower-middle class existence depended on my father's position. He was not a mailman, not one of those healthy, cheerful fixtures of suburban life, smiling and waving through every type of weather. No, my father was a clerk, a sorter. It was his lonely job to meet the mail truck at an ungodly morning hour and then sort the letters, advertising and packages—by hand, back in those days—so that they would be ready for delivery at first light. He did not wear a uniform. He was thin and pale, awake at two in the morning and asleep by seven in the evening. On most days I would see him briefly just before supper, just long enough to exchange a hello. The result is that he is conspicuously absent from my childhood memories. I was raised—whatever that means—by my mother. And she doted on me. She was selfless. She did everything in her power to make me happy. Despite our modest circumstances I cannot recall a single instance of deprivation. All in all my early years were quite pleasant, quite pleasant indeed.

Thanks to a confluence of luck and genetics I was an exceptional student. Learning came easily. And I was taught early not to squander my gifts. I worked hard but enjoyed my studies. My bookishness stultified any errant attempts at a social life. This sacrifice, however, paid dividends when I received a full scholarship to the university. I was the first person on either side of the family to enter the world of higher education. This fact, if you can believe it, made me even more studious.

That was my youth, I'm afraid. There were no seminal moments or rites of passage. I recall no psychological trauma. I wasn't bullied or abused. I just grew older, normally. Now, I am but a simple layman, however I feel my sketch was not as fruitful as you had hoped. Perhaps you are reserving judgment. Perhaps you are processing the story in ways I could not begin to imagine. For all I know I may have innocently provided you with a significant detail or two among what I would deem years of insignificance. I don't know. Nor do I know why I continue with these editorial asides.

So, if I may continue with my life, we are about to reach what we would both—here, I believe, it is safe to assume—what we would both consider a noteworthy moment. Shortly after I entered my final year at university my mother announced that she was pregnant. My parents had been, as was the norm for their generation, relatively young when they married and my mother was just twenty-two when I was born. Two decades later, a few weeks before I graduated summa cum laude, I became a brother, a much, much older brother, to a sister my parents named Karen. I will leave you to ascertain the impact of such a development on a young man's psyche, but it would be unfair to characterize the irregular relationship as that of siblings. The age difference was too great. Over the years I was more of an uncle than a brother.

I was a stranger to her, a reluctant, and I suspect, unwelcome infrequent guest. Karen failed to follow in my academic footsteps and upon high school graduation she became a waitress at a local diner. Soon thereafter my parents—their child-rearing responsibilities finished—passed away within a year of each other: my father from an aneurysm and my mother from what Karen and I initially called a broken heart, but what was in actuality an aggressive cancer of the pancreas. My career was my main focus at the time and it was going well. I offered assistance, financial and other, to my sister but she declined dismissively. Most likely my suggestions carried the scent of charity, an inelegant offer more hurtful than protective. After that we did not speak very often, a détente that seemed to work for us both. I was named CEO the same week Karen phoned to tell me that she was pregnant. At first she wouldn't speak of the father. I later learned that he was a motorcyclist, a diner regular, who was killed in a traffic accident shortly after impregnating my sister. I was at my sister's side when her daughter was born. I like to think that I even had a small hand in her naming—I suggested Fern, she chose Heather. Over the years I have done what I could to support them both. It has been an uneasy dynamic. In reality I am brother and uncle, yet age and experience make me appear and act like uncle and grandfather. Despite my general tactlessness I felt it was my duty to support them. I did what I could. My influence, however, had its limits. Heather possessed my scholarly aptitude and controlling nature—when she was a little girl I often

115

watched her play with others, all she did was talk, ordering her friends here and there, it was *you pretend this* and *you pretend that*, that was how she played—but when the time came she turned her back on my offer to pay for university. She did, though, accept my offer of employment. In retrospect I should have made the offer conditional on continuing her education but it would after all have been unparalleled impertinence to offer her a position and then conditionally rescind the offer. I suspect it would have made me appear too cold and calculating. No. And there we are. That is my family. As you can see I am not as alone as advertised. Heather, I assume, is still employed at AGE and her mother, my unmarried, middle-aged sister Karen, has, apart from her brief maternity leave, never to my knowledge missed her regular shift at the diner.

All this talk of family has suddenly made me feel older than my years. I am a sorrowing old man. *Sorrowing*. Did you notice my slip? No. I meant to say sorrowful yet I said sorrowing. Isn't that the kind of apparent triviality you psychotherapists deem important? Me? I don't know. I think it's probably important because it was a glimpse into my unconscious. You see *Sorrowing Old Man* is the title of a Van Gogh painting, so my error I expect was evocative of the piece. The work also goes by the title of *Worn Out: At Eternity's Gate*. I don't know. It might resonate for many reasons. It was a reworking of earlier drawings. Van Gogh came to do the piece because of the shortage of inspiration within the four walls of Saint-Remy's Asylum where he was convalescing. Sound familiar? It depicts an old man on a chair crying for unknown reasons, his eyes concealed behind clenched fists. The old man wears all blue but for worn brown shoes, a small fire burns behind him. It might show the old man sorrowing for his misery as he nears death—contrast this with Gaugin's old woman with the white bird. Van Gogh used the image to capture his own mental state in decline. It represents the uncertainty of all humanity. The artist told people that the painting illustrated belief in something on high. My malapropism may be related to any, all or none of this.

Do I fear my own death? Don't you? We mustn't pretend to ourselves. We may keel over at any moment. Someone once wrote: Everyone wants to be alive, nobody wants to die. Everything else is a lie. No, I am not attempting to deflect. And I am not being flippant. I do not know. If I am being truthful then I would have to answer in the affirmative. Allow me to add, however, that I do not believe in absolutes. And these opposing forces, I suppose, add up to a more nuanced, conflicted answer to your question. In the final analysis I fear the unknown more than I fear death. Have you ever heard of those who report so-called near death experiences, the fortunate souls who see shining light and friendly faces and feel so warm and fuzzy about dying that they are returned to life? I realize that for many reasons I am in no position to pass judgment. Even so, a number of scientists believe they have the explanation for this so-called experience. Their novel theory is that our self-conception—what we believe makes us us—requires so much brain power that as one is dying—when actual cellular and neuronal death has begun—one may experience a disconnectedness and this disconnectedness is what these 'dead' people are reporting. And of course the reason they generally tend to report the same experiences is because they generally share the same belief systems, so what they see is what they expected to see. The theory, if true, means we might all have a self-fulfilling death prophecy. This frightens me even more.

No, that is not true; my concluding statement was in jest. No, on my deathbed just before I give up the ghost—a splendid phrase, don't you think?—I do not expect to see my life flash before my eyes. I do not expect to relive the past. I harbor few illusions of epiphany. I imagine that my waning strength might allow me a few moments to mourn the future, a future without me as witness. That will be my tragedy. I will envision this future in a haze of painkillers and confusion. And my dreamlike vision of what the world will be when I'm gone will slowly unveil itself as my defeated consciousness loses its final battle.

Forgive me, I now find this subject morbid and distasteful. Perhaps I am a little too close. Allow me to change to a more pleasant topic.

I hope you will be encouraged by my progress when I announce that I participated in group therapy yesterday. I do not mean that I merely attended. No, by participation I mean that I spoke at the session. It wasn't much but it was a first. If you'll indulge me I will describe how this came to be.

The usual suspects—those who enjoy the sound

of their own voice—were blathering in their usual manner while Doolittle and I whispered wittily to each other. At one point one of the usual suspects—there is no point in naming the poor man—launched into a lengthy exposition on his Catholicism and how his religion had helped him better cope with his mental illness. In the middle of the nameless man's stupid dialogue Doolittle stood and shouted, *Transubstantiation!* I warned you that he was quite mad. Before I was able to coax him back into his chair—and those metal chairs, by the way, are as uncomfortable as ever; I am still waiting for my cushion, though, to tell the truth I half suspect my request will never be granted under the rationale that it would somehow endanger the egalitarian climate considered so critical to the group dynamic—excuse me, where was I? Doolittle. Before I managed to get Doolittle to sit down he had rifled off a series of bullet questions aimed at the man and the Catholic Church. His last question—*Do you truly believe the wafer that you are eating is the real body of Christ?*—provoked a response. *Yes, that is what I believe. It is the key to my faith,* said the man. Doolittle seemed satisfied and he sat down. But before the man could continue in his defense of Catholicism, Doolittle said loudly: *Interesting. The sewer rats have a similar belief. But they believe ALL food is sacred embodiment, not just consecrated slices of unleavened bread.* Stifling a laugh and fearing the man might physically attack my friend it was at this juncture I intervened to defuse the diffuse situation. I do not remember precisely what I said but it was something to the effect that vermin and Catholics and everybody else on this planet has an inherent right to their own private beliefs as long as these beliefs do not harm or threaten others. *The only universal belief is belief itself*, I said. The group leader thanked me for my calming words of unity and the session, though perceptibly strained, continued for the remainder of the allotted time. I know it may not seem like much and, indeed, it was performed in the express hope of protecting my friend but I would like to think my participation represents a milestone in my recovery.

I am happy to hear you agree. One continually questions one's own perceptions in this place. Of course I am delighted, though the phrase *barring any setbacks* looms threateningly. Still and all, the knowledge that my release may be close at hand is wonderful news. I suspect Doolittle will be thrilled for me.

Another excellent question. I have been so concentrated on my recovery that I have not spent much time contemplating what I might do upon my release. No, money is not at issue. What I have will suffice for as long as I live. What could be next for me? It is difficult to imagine an existence outside the world of gears. They have been my life. But clearly a return to AGE is impossible. The manner and events of my departure preclude it. Even were I encouraged it would be degrading, somehow emasculating. I would be forever reproaching myself. It would be indefensible. Surely there are other opportunities in the field, with a manufacturer perhaps. Yet word of my illness and actions must have traveled. It is a small community. Perhaps everyone thinks me no longer capable. My reputation may have been irreparably damaged. A break from the industry might be in order. A not-so-clean break. I have always wondered what it would be like to spend my time among great art. Maybe I could work or volunteer at a museum. The prospect is intriguing. I do not have to make my decision now, do I? It is not a prerequisite to my release, is it?

At a minimum—though we both know that I lack the necessary temperament—I feel I should attempt to repair the relationships with my sister and Heather. We are, after all, family. The fact that neither has visited me during my stay here should not be used as an excuse. I am no one's burden. Besides who knows how badly I may have treated them during the progression of my illness. Apologies may be in order. My sister and I are not getting younger and we are both, to the best of my knowledge, alone. And Heather is just entering adulthood. Surely I could be of some service to her. Doctor she is incredibly beautiful and clever but conceals her beauty and intelligence behind mourning clothes and nihilism or some such philosophical nonsense. She speaks like a learned mortician. It is as if she has given up on life before even starting. She is too young to be so sad. And she is too pretty to be alone. I would like the opportunity to cheer her up if possible, if she would allow me. At the very least I could be a cautionary exemplar of disease and detachment, couldn't I? Ah, but these are only speculations. For now I have my indigestion-inducing medicine and my therapy. The future is another day.

SPUR

The time had come, thought Tom. I need to do it. I need to ask her out. It'll be weird if I don't. It's either a real relationship or it isn't. It's time to know. One date, one night. But, how? When? There weren't enough hours in the day.

Timing is crucial, in gears and in life. And both gears and life had joined forces to conspire against him. Gearkegaard hadn't been seen in weeks—rumor had it that he was at the university using their state of the art three-dimensional printer to manufacture Great Gear prototypes—which meant that he and Sid were forced to pick up the consulting slack. It was too much for two people. It was too much for three people unless one of the three was Gearkegaard. It was much too much. Too many gears, too many things in motion. And all he could think about was Sobs, how work kept him from her, how he missed her. How close he'd been. Now he felt he was retrogressing. He'd even caught Corey sniffing around again. He was stressed. One date, one night.

Sam told Sobs that whatever she decided was fine by him.

I don't give a fig about pattern. I don't give a fig about color. I don't give a fig about shape. As long as it sticks and has room for a name, it's good enough for me. It's a NAMETAG.

It was not what she wanted to hear. She wanted him to choose or at the very least validate her choice. That way she couldn't make the wrong decision. Really. A wrong nametag recommendation? Seriously? Sometimes she almost laughed out loud. How did this happen? When? The Ear's insidious grand plan had done its damage. It had turned a simple single assignment into something else. Her one measly responsibility had assumed mammoth importance. It was beyond comical. And now she was afraid. She was afraid to pick a nametag. She was paralyzed. Her quest for the perfect nametag had taken on mythic proportions. It had become more than an objective, more than an assignment, more than a nametag. It had become meaningful. Yuck, she thought. It had become significant. How? When?

I'm pathetic, Sobs said. She didn't know whether to laugh or cry.

Rita ran around with an oversized birthday card getting signatures. Matt was turning twenty-three.

Write something nice, she begged Corey. Poor Matt hasn't been the same since D.C.

Cake at three, she reminded.

Tyler had selected the Merry Manatee Hotel and Resort for the annual conference. Sam's minimal requirements—someplace warm that won't run out of alcohol, by a nice beach, if possible—had been met. The beachfront property on Buffett Island off Florida's southwest coast ticked the boxes.

It has the best shelling beaches in the country, touted Tyler, shoving a bright brochure in Sobs' face.

Who cares about shelling? Tyler, I've got my own problems here. Can you get that out of my face?

I'll have you know that shelling is one of the fastest growing pastimes in the United States, he said. Young, old, rich, poor, everybody enjoys a good seashell. And did you know that a good shell can be worth hundreds of dollars, thousands even? See, read this: Every shell possesses its own unique enigmatic beauty. And look at the pool. Imagine me beside that pool, bronzing. Ooh, it gives me chills.

Tyler—

Lordy, somebody woke up on the wrong side of the coffin. Tell me Elvira, what's troubling you? And it better not be the nametag again, because I will lose my—

I can't decide.

Oh, for God's sake, give me that.

Tyler took the catalogue and flicked through it umming and icking. Then he stopped.

Here, this one. It does not possess unique enigmatic beauty, but it'll work with the resort logo.

Not bad. But—

You're welcome. Now back to me bronzing.

Sam, I have a surprise for you, said the Ear.

Sam smiled weakly. Experience taught him that surprises mean more work.

Your conference, *our* conference, is going to make history.

Super, said Sam.

You've heard of the Great Gear, I assume.

A little, I suppose.

The Ear laughed. A little, yes, that's good. There is nothing little about it. Sam this will change the world.

And what does that have to do with me?

The Great Gear will be unveiled, revealed to the world if you will, at your conference.

It will?

It will. Isn't that exciting? You are a very lucky man. You will be organizing a once in a lifetime event. Yes. So, I'll need you to arrange everything. It has to be big. It should be on the final afternoon of the conference before the important attendees start to head home. Get in touch with the media. We want a big turnout. Spare no expense. It should be large, lavish. Contact Lars to coordinate. He has certain technical requirements. I'll leave you in charge of the details.

Sam scribbled on his notepad pretending to take notes. He drew various sized spirals and thought about sipping whiskey while the Ear talked and talked.

I must confess that your alluring photo stopped me dead in my tracks. I was floored. You are stunning.

After what seemed forever, I finally caught my breath and perused your profile. It's kismet. We have the same interests, similar likes and dislikes—e.g. I, too, enjoy fine dining and meaty Cabernet Sauvignons. To be honest it all appears too good to be true. But I am willing to risk it. All evidence points to you being an intelligent, fun, beautiful, interesting and sexy lady. I would love the opportunity to get to know you better. Please peruse my profile and let me know if you think there might be something here—SensitiveStud45

Gwen clicked her mouse on the link to read SensitiveStud45's profile. She froze at the photo. Shirtless, he held what appeared to be a white baby rabbit in the crook of his arm.

Grant cleared his throat. It was five minutes before noon.

Oh, I am so sorry. I. Oh my, I didn't hear you come in. I am sorry. I was just. I do apologize, stammered Gwen. Sorry. How may I help you?

I'm here to see Blair Hunt. I believe I'm expected.

Your name?

Grant. Grant Icahn.

Please have a seat, Mr. Icahn. I'm sure Ms. Hunt will be down shortly.

Grant strolled around the reception area. Gwen called Blair.

Blair, I knew it, she whispered. He is dreamy. And he's here waiting for you. Take your time.

Grant studied the industry awards lining the walls. Gwen studied Grant. She wondered what he'd look like holding a bunny.

Now it's your turn to help me, said Tyler, time to scratch my back. I love how this tit-for-tat works. What do you know about this Great Gear? How great is it? Is it really big?

I don't even think that it's real, answered Sobs. And if it is I don't care.

Care for me, then, will you? There's going to be a mega show-and-tell at the conference. I have to produce. How can I get in touch with Gearkegaard? I need information.

How would I know?

Hello! Engineer Tom Von Smitten practically lives at your desk. He must know. Ask him.

I—

Just have your boyfriend send me his boss's contact info. Please.

He's not my—

TMI. Contact info, please and thank you.

Blair chose a busy café around the corner for their lunch. She picked at a soggy Caesar salad while Grant pushed overcooked pasta primavera around his plate.

So what's the latest in Washington?

Oh, you know, wars, waste and wish lists. Same as ever, said Grant. Only the names change.

You can't fool me. I know you like it.

Never said I didn't like it. And what about you? Why aren't you there? Seems K Street would be your kind of neighborhood.

Perhaps one day, said Blair. I'd like to think that my career is still on an upward trajectory. Anything is possible. In truth she'd always aspired to K Street. It was the big leagues for lobbyists, the MBA Promised Land. She felt that Grant understood her dream. And she was okay with that. He was a good person to have on her side.

Well, if there's anything I can ever do, ask. I know many people on many streets.

Sam hopped off a nearby barstool and made his way toward their booth.

Hide, said Blair, ducking slightly.

What?

Blair, boomed Sam, and . . . I don't believe I've had the pleasure.

Grant, Sam. Sam, Grant.

Nice to meet you.

Likewise.

Just wanted to say hello, be neighborly and all that.

Would you care to join us?

No, I couldn't, but thank you very much for the invitation. My sustenance is over there. Nice meeting you. Blair.

They both watched Sam weave back to the bar.

Who was that? asked Grant.

That was Sam. A coworker. He's the conference guy. A walking disaster. Let's just say that he's not a bit puzzled about what to do when he finds a glass of whiskey in his hands.

Right. Got it.

They're not like us, Grant. Not a single one of them. They're idiots. They are all idiots. There's something fundamentally wrong with them. Did you know that my boss—we call him the Ear—blames me for what happened in Washington? His behavior is my fault. He said I hadn't prepared him properly. He blames me. Me. He actually said that my performance was unsatisfactory. My performance has never been unsatisfactory . . . in anything.

Maybe K Street is closer than you think.

After the meal, Grant insisted on seeing the Ear. Blair thought it might earn her needed points.

He should be available, said Magda. You know how I hate scheduling appointments on a Tuesday, said Magda fingering her *mati*.

What's with Tuesdays? whispered Grant.

Don't ask.

You can go right in.

The Ear was pleased to see Grant. He welcomed him with his best smile.

Good to see you again. What brings you to our neck of the woods?

Oh, nothing really, I had a layover and wanted to stop by to tell Blair that her gear manufacturing message was gaining substantial traction, at least in the Senate. There's talk about a possible legislation.

Wonderful. Wonderful.

Blair looked at Grant and almost winked.

So where do you keep that super gear? asked Grant. Is it locked away in a super vault?

The Great Gear? No, said the Ear laughing. It's not under lock and key. We are in the process of constructing prototypes. There's work yet to be done. I will, however, let you in on something that isn't public yet. We plan to unveil the Great Gear at our upcoming conference in Florida. It'll be a major event. Why don't you attend? I'll see that you get the details. We'd love to have you and the senator at the event.

That is very nice. I'll be sure to pass along the invitation to Senator Archer. Perhaps we could get a sneak peek before the unveiling? Help sell it to the senator.

Oh, I don't know about that. Our engineers are leading the effort. I do not micromanage my staff. I'm about the big picture. I stay out of the minutiae.

Blair, why don't you take him over to consulting and design and have him talk with Sid and Tom. They're better equipped to answer your questions.

That would be enlightening. Thank you.

It was a pleasure seeing you again. My best to the senator.

Neither Tom nor Sid knew any more about the Great Gear than the Ear. Initially Grant thought they might be stonewalling.

Our boss is the lead on this one. We've been focused on the day-to-day consulting end of the business.

At one point Tom took Blair aside and admitted that they hadn't seen Gearkegaard in weeks.

Blair brusquely terminated the question/non-answer session by announcing she had just remembered an important conference call starting in a few minutes. She would see Grant out.

Gwen leaped from behind the reception desk and

snatched Grant's ringless left hand.

It was heavenly to have you here with us. It's delightful to see a new face. Things can get pretty predictable here in the gear world.

Thank you, Gwen, said Blair.

Maybe I'll see you at the conference? We all go, you know. Close the offices. Florida this year. Sun and sea. Everybody will be there.

Conceivably, said Grant, rescuing his hand.

Blair walked him to the door.

I don't know why you came, but thank you.

The pleasure was mine. I hope we meet again and soon.

Two days later, Gwen looked up from Sinplicity7's dating profile to see Larry Chi Lun waiting patiently.

Yes, now, how may I assist you?

A minute passed before Magda trundled in and greeted Larry with a sincere smile.

Mr. Chi Lun, you made it. No problems finding us, I hope.

No, your directions were quite specific. I did get a little lost searching for an ATM.

Oh, those ATMs, I don't believe in them myself. Never have.

She took Larry by the arm and led him toward the Ear's office. Larry wondered how someone could not believe in ATMs. They exist, he thought, what's not to believe.

Gwen's gaze returned to her computer. She did not see them leave.

Ah, a Raygon representative, said the Ear flashing his megawatt whites. It is always a treat meeting one of our partners and benefactors. Come to see how we're spending your money? Joking, just joking. Please have a seat, Mr. Chi Lun. What can I do for you?

Larry justified his presence by manufacturing a story that he was in the area on unrelated business and thought a visit would be an interesting field trip. AGE had been assisting his work for years. He hoped to express his gratitude to the engineers and others.

Certainly, said the Ear, whatever you would like. We appreciate the compliment. Such feedback is invaluable. Few make the effort to deliver such messages in person. I thank you. And may I add that you have arrived at a, well, call it fate or good luck, but you have arrived at a very interesting time.

Have I?

You have. Soon, very, very soon, we will announce a major breakthrough in gear design. Not to sound immodest, you are an engineer after all, but I would deem it the final word in gear design. The last gear humanity will ever need. Design perfection. We call it the Great Gear.

Larry was mum. He didn't feel like a spy. He felt like a child on his birthday.

Difficult to comprehend, I know, continued the Ear. But I assure you it exists. It is real. We plan on making the announcement at our annual conference.

I don't know what to say.

That's how I felt too. It takes time to sink in. It's hard to believe. I don't mean to overwhelm you, but since you and Raygon are part of the AGE family I feel comfortable sharing something else.

Thank you. Yes. Please.

Our announcement will include all the necessary specifications and designs for the open manufacture of the Great Gear. We are making it free to everyone. It is our present to the planet. All the patents will be available for use by anyone. Not to be corny, but we hope to usher in a new AGE.

That is quite generous.

Such inventions belong to the world, said the Ear leaning back in his chair. Some ideas are too big for private ownership.

Extraordinary.

Stunned, Larry was also relieved. It was a strange feeling. If true, his assignment was over. No need to rebalance equilibrium if the technology is free and open. But he was also concerned that it sounded too good to be true. A motive was missing.

You mentioned that you wanted to talk to engineers. Let's start there. Magda, would you please come in and escort Mr. Chi Lun to consulting and design?

The tour was a blur. Larry tried to imagine what a perfect gear would look like while Magda hustled him from office to bland office hissing *skorda* under her breath at various intervals.

In engineering Sid and Tom apologized for Gearkegaard's absence. They'd never seen the Great Gear. Everything was kept offsite, who knows where.

At conferences, Tyler tried to upsell Larry and Raygon for the big conference.

An extra table for you and your colleagues. Right up front. You don't want to miss the big event. When I work with your company I usually work with Helen Mills. Do you know her? She's marvelous. Now, I wouldn't want to do anything without her approval, but there's no harm in us talking, is there?

Larry left with a vague promise to check his schedule and talk to Helen whom he did not know.

He suffered through a slice of stale birthday cake.

Corey and Matt, the birthday boy, confused an uninterested Larry with messages about messaging and talk about traction.

At the end of the long day, alone, in his little red rental car, Larry didn't know what to think. He wasn't sure if there was a problem to solve. He phoned his wife and said that he'd be on the first flight in the morning.

Sobs passed the catalogue to Gwen and pointed. Tyler's suggestion was circled in green.

What do you think?

It's—

If you don't like it, Tyler picked it out.

No, it's not that I don't like it. It's just that it's a nametag. Hard to have a favorite.

Yeah, Sam said the same.

Though this one here would go nicely with the new blouse I bought. It really accentuates my boobs—the blouse, not the nametag.

Sobs almost laughed.

Are you sure this is just about a nametag?

Yes. No. Maybe. I don't know. I don't know what the hell is happening to me.

Gwen swiveled her computer monitor toward Sobs.

What you need is this.

Really? MaxThrust69?

Look at that jawline. And those abs. And look lower. Ooh.

What's wrong with me? thought Sobs. What's wrong? Why hasn't he asked me out?

HELICAL

Meteorologists call it a forecast. It is a prediction by another name, a prediction cloaked in statistics and maps, modeling and climatology. It is a guess. And when, as often happens, the guess proves inaccurate the meteorologists employ the same methodologies, the same maps, models and climatology to explain why the guess was wrong. An inexact science is not science.

District of Columbia meteorologists called for cool temperatures and clear skies. It was warm and wet. Grant briefed Senator Archer on the AGE trip.

It's a circus—he had almost said zoo—Senator. No one knows what's going on. Briar is certifiable. The guy's a nut job. They call him the Ear. Apparently the only one he listens to is God. The lead engineer is some kind of ancient, mysterious elf or hobbit, always MIA. An angry, sardonic Indian is in charge of design. The conference guy is a drunk. The receptionist is a sexual predator. It's a circus, sir. Blair

Hunt is the only normal one in the whole bunch.

A circus, you say.

And I am not exaggerating. If they do have something, it's sheer luck. I don't even know how these people have jobs. If they do possess this Great Gear, it is most definitely in the wrong hands.

Human beings are interesting animals, began the senator. We believe we're unique. Did you know that chimpanzees are the only other primates that murder their own? We used to think their murderous impulse came from human interference and that we taught them to kill. As it turns out the practice results from normal competition. It's coded in their DNA. And in ours.

Senator, I don't—

Darwin's tubercle. Check the ear.

Sir—

Get the gear, Grant. Whatever it takes. If it's in the wrong hands, let's put it in the right ones.

The weather outside the AGE offices was cool and clear. Local meteorologists had called for warm and wet. The Ear spoke to Gearkegaard over the telephone.

Do your best. That's all any of us can do, he said.

They will be ready for the unveiling. Guaranteed.

I am concerned that there won't be enough time for testing. We would be assuming substantial risk demonstrating transmissions that have not been properly vetted.

They work, said Gearkegaard. They will work.

It is out of my hands. Faith will be rewarded. Do

your best and be onsite as soon as humanly possible.

The Ear replaced the receiver. There must be a reason, he thought.

It was another sunny, dry day in California. Meteorologists there were on a winning streak. For the twenty-third day in a row they had forecast sunny, dry weather. For the twenty-third day in a row they had been correct.

Larry looked out the spotless picture window and wondered whether his grass needed another coat of paint. The phone rang. A male Chinese voice, different than the first, but interchangeable, said that his mission must continue. There are worries that the open-source unveiling might be a trick, said the voice. Attend the ceremony, investigate and verify.

Peggy will not be happy about this, thought Larry.

The forecast for Florida was bad, very bad. A category four hurricane named Mary was on her way. Buffett Island and the Merry Manatee Hotel and Resort were in her angry path.

We have to postpone the conference, Sam told the Ear.

There is no need to do that. Don't worry.

Look, I'm as devil-may-care as anyone, but it's a hurricane.

The hurricane will not strike our hotel.

The weatherman says otherwise.

It will be fine.

Don't you understand? No one will come. The

storm will scare them off. Even if we don't get hit, there'll be nobody there. We'll be lucky to get fifty people there. We need to reschedule.

We cannot do that. The conference is to go on as planned. Do your job and don't worry about Mary.

It's your call. You're the boss.

Have faith, Sam. Have faith.

Larry was concerned about the forecast in Florida so he booked a flight a day early to be on the safe side. Peggy didn't think it was safe.

There's a hurricane on the way.

I'll be fine.

It's a conference.

It's an important conference.

The Annual Gear Manufacturer's Conference was scheduled for Thursday and Friday. Most attendees would therefore arrive for their complimentary cocktail on Wednesday afternoon or evening. Speakers and breakout sessions were to be held all day Thursday and Friday morning. Guests were on their own for Thursday lunch, but a large evening banquet, featuring filet mignon and lobster followed by authentic key lime pie, was planned for dinner. After the feast attendees would be invited to the open bar. Continental breakfast would be available both mornings between seven and nine. A special lunch would be provided on Friday. Sam hoped the free lunch would funnel more people into the Great Gear presentation.

To prepare, AGE staff arranged to fly in on Tuesday, despite Magda's third day of the week trepidation. As they boarded the plane meteorologists believed that Hurricane Mary had an eighty percent chance of making landfall in southwest Florida.

Tom felt free, finally. The conference would be a paid vacation, a well-deserved rest. All he had to do was help out when asked, direct Great Gear questions to Gearkegaard and have fun. He was going to seize the moment.

Sobs sat in twenty-two B, across the aisle. She wore black earbuds. She was so close. He wanted to take her hand. Too public, he thought. She might not want him to. She might slap him, though he considered that prospect unlikely. We'll have time together in Florida. She won't be that busy. All she's got is nametags. We'll have time together, he told himself. When the moment comes, I will seize it.

Sam had been slightly over-served during the flight so Tyler took over when they landed. He directed everyone everywhere. Sam was happy to abdicate responsibility. Soon, after efficiently locating luggage and securing taxis, they alighted at the Merry Manatee.

From above, the resort complex looked like a giant division sign: two round residential towers separated by a salt-stained rectilinear slash containing reception, conference rooms, dining areas and the bar. At ground level the low middle line, slouching between the twin honeycombed towers, seemed like a junior architect's afterthought. A giant, smiling, pink manatee, obviously very merry from all the sun, sea, surf and sand, greeted them from the flapping front entrance awning.

As the others checked-in, Tyler buzzed around the pastel lobby rearranging the arrangements.

These people wouldn't know flowers if they bit them in the ass, he said.

At the Queen Motel, a mile and a half down the beach from the Merry Manatee, Larry read a crime novel in room 212. His flight had arrived two hours earlier. He had decided to lay low for a night. He felt it would be suspicious if he arrived before the other attendees. He didn't want to appear too eager.

The Ear and his staff spent Tuesday getting acclimated to the hotel and the thickening tropical air. Work and cloud cover prevented Tyler from tanning. Tom asked Sid if he'd heard from Gearkegaard. Magda worried about the storm. Sobs unpacked her nametags. Sam had a drink with Corey and Gwen at the bar. Rita took pre-conference photos. Matt sulked.

On Wednesday morning the National Hurricane Service announced that Mary had a ninety percent chance of hitting southwest Florida. The governor requested local voluntary evacuation.

The Ear told everyone not to worry.

The storm will not strike us. Have faith. It's just scaremongering.

A few conference attendees arrived. Gwen, Magda and Sobs greeted them in the lobby and gave them each a crisp AGE folder containing a free ballpoint pen. Sobs handed out nametags.

The clouds swelled biblically. The Ear maintained that there was nothing to worry about.

Late afternoon the local airport closed. Sam explained the situation to the Ear.

Well, that's it then. No more conference. I warned you that we should have postponed.

That is not it. People have already arrived. The conference will go on. The storm will not disrupt us.

But nobody can get here.

That is your problem. It is your job to make this conference a success. It is your job to ensure that we have an adequate turnout.

I can't control the weather, said Sam.

I've told you that the storm will not hit us. Now forget about the weather and concentrate your energies on the conference. Remember your objectives. That's your job.

Unable to fly direct, Grant flew to Atlanta, rented a car and pointed it toward Buffett Island and the approaching hurricane. As he drove through the Florida flatness, he thought about Blair, the Great Gear and Hurricane Mary. Woman, invention, storm. Each one a mystery. He realized he was anxious, maybe even excited. He hadn't felt this way in a very long time. His speed increased.

Okay. See you tomorrow. Drive carefully, said Blair.

Who was that? You should have seen your face, said Gwen.

Oh, nobody. Grant. The guy from Washington. He'll be here tomorrow. He's driving.

He must really want to see you.

I don't think it's me.

So there's nothing between you two? Then you won't mind if I have a go.

On Wednesday evening Larry checked into the Merry Manatee. Sobs was the only one at the conference welcome table.

Mr. Chi Lun. Raygon. And all the way from California. How'd you get here with the airport closed?

Larry told her that his nephew lived nearby. He arrived a few days ago to spend some time with him. Sobs nodded and gave him three nametags: one for Larry, one for Chi and one for Lun. She had plenty of nametags.

The Merry Manatee's general manager pulled Sam aside and explained that due to the storm staffing may become a problem.

I have to put my people's safety first, he said.

I understand, said Sam. I don't think we're going to have numbers anyway. Just do me a favor and make sure we don't run out of bartenders.

I'll get behind the bar myself if I have to.

Has anyone heard from Lars? asked the Ear.

Not a single one of the invited speakers had made it. Sam counted twenty-seven total attendees, including AGE staff. Over four hundred had registered. Sam gave the bad news to the Ear.

Most are local, from here in Florida. We have a couple from Georgia and Alabama and one guy from California. I'll be damned if I know how he got here. But that's it. So what do you want me to do?

Do your best, Sam. I expect you to do your best. Adversity challenges us to be our best. Welcome them. Make sure they enjoy themselves. Do your best for Thursday. And remember that Friday is another day. Things can change rapidly.

Tyler had arranged a personal private preview of Thursday's surf and turf dinner.

To ensure that everything is presentable, if not eatable, he told the others.

Despite a suspicion that ordinary rather than key limes had been used in the dessert, Tyler concluded the chef had done an adequate job. He wiped his lips' corner with an ecru napkin and nodded with satisfaction. Then he dragged himself to the fitness room and jogged on a treadmill for three point two miles. A fat bronze god is not a god, he thought. As if to prove the point the only other person he saw working out was an obese salesman from Alabama who pushed random buttons on an elliptical machine for a minute or two then left. Tired and sated, Tyler went to bed early.

Sid, has Lars been in touch? asked the Ear. I haven't

heard from him. Have we received any packages? He said he was shipping as soon as possible.

The bar at the Merry Manatee was called Cousin Dugong's. It was a typical tiki lounge. The ceiling was bamboo, the chairs rattan. Umbrella drinks were the specialty. Corey called for another Singapore sling. The bartender presented the cocktail and turned up the television volume.

The National Hurricane Center now predicts with ninety-five percent certainty that Mary will make landfall at or near Buffett Island off Florida's southwest coast.

Corey looked forward to the storm. Anything to spice it up, he thought. I should be swimming in women by now. This place is dead. Nobody here but the usual idiots.

Gwen, Matt, Sid and Sam joined Corey at the bar. They watched television and placed bets on whether Gearkegaard would make it by Friday afternoon.

And they drank. They drank because there was nothing else to do. They drank because they liked it. They drank to be alone, together: to bind their loneliness to all other lonelinesses.

Some conference, said Gwen, it's more like a glorified pajama party, no offense Sam.

None taken. You're preaching to the choir. I told the Ear we should've cancelled.

After his fifth beer Matt turned to Sam and put his arm around him.

You conference people are the best.

Sure we are, kid. Sure we are.

Poolside, Sobs and Tom tried to talk. The intensifying winds swirled their words making it difficult to tell who said what.

I've wanted to talk to you.

Me too.

Things have been so hectic lately.

We should go out on a proper date.

I've missed you.

I used to look forward to work.

I should've been around more.

I should be more patient.

It hasn't been fair. Has it?

I really like you.

Hey, check out those gnarly waves! shouted Corey breaking the wind's spell. Surf is most definitely up.

Tom shook his head.

I can't see anything, said Sobs.

No, but you can hear them. You don't have to see them. You can hear how big they are.

It began to rain. Sobs and Tom dashed into the resort. Corey cursed the skies.

Bring it, Mary. Let's see what you've got.

Tom walked Sobs to her door, said good night, thought about leaning in for a kiss then thought too much about it, and ultimately settled for repeating good night a second time before watching her close the door. He retired to his room and tried to fall asleep.

Sopping, Corey returned to Cousin Dugong's for another drink. Blair followed his wobbly walk. Gwen sidled next to Blair and asked.

What's he like, your Grant? What's he really like? He seems dreamy.

Blair ordered a Tanqueray and tonic and told Gwen everything she knew about Grant the spy. Gwen was impressed.

You're sure you two aren't an item.

Pretty sure, answered Blair. Pretty sure.

In that case I need my beauty sleep, said Gwen.

I'll go up with you.

Bored and gallant, Sid escorted the two women to their rooms.

The Ear fell asleep early comforted by and confident in the knowledge that the Lord wasn't going to let a hurricane—especially one named after His virgin mother—ruin the Great Gear announcement.

Corey passed out in his bathroom, pants around his ankles.

Hour after hour the storm got stronger. The lights flickered on and off and on. The wind moaned and howled in the darkness.

Frightened, Magda cowered in her room sorting and resorting bat bones by flashlight.

Tyler dreamt of tanning in the warm sunlight while muscular hands fed him fat grapes.

Rita read and wrote and contemplated the storm. An approaching hurricane would be a wonderful device to heighten tension in my narrative, she thought.

Larry lay awake listening to the rain. It sounded foreign to his California ears. His wished he could transport it back home. He thought about Peggy and his two girls. He thought about how pleasant his life had turned out. And, as he drifted off to sleep, he imagined an enormous Great Gear assembly turning in the clouds.

Tom dreamed of Sobs and Sobs dreamed of Tom. They cursed Corey and missed opportunities; neither slept very well.

Matt and Sam stayed and drank at Cousin Dugong's until it closed.

Thicker raindrops fell. The wind whipped wildly.

And then, at five minutes to three ante meridiem Eastern Standard Time, Mary turned sharply west. She raced into the middle of the gulf and unraveled her considerable strength over open water. The Ear had been right.

Thursday morning the meteorologists scrambled to explain the phenomenon. One reported that a freak cold front from Canada had turned Mary. Another claimed that gulf surface water temperatures due to excessive algae growth caused her sudden course change. One even called it an unexplainable miracle. Each and every one of them said that never in their career had they seen such behavior from a hurricane. It was unprecedented.

But it still rained. It was still gray outside. And inside there was nothing to do. The mood was black. The resort was almost empty. It was a ghost resort. The manager had, in a cost-saving move, closed one of the towers. Attendees and staff picked at the continental breakfast and talked about the storm that wasn't. They were safe, but bored, stranded and shipwrecked. Sid laughed saying that they had all been manateed.

Sam organized a morning Q and A session. Few attended. And only two questions were asked:

When will the airport reopen so I can get out of here?

and

Are you still going to show us the Great Gear?

In good conscience Sam couldn't answer either question.

Tyler appeared in the afternoon draped and dripping in nametags, head to toe, back to front. He had colored them brown and told everyone who asked that he was sporting a tan, albeit a Crayola one. Here and there nametags dropped littering lobby and hallways. Sobs scrambled to pick them up before the Ear noticed.

Unseen, Grant pulled up to reception in a small blue

rental car. He was oddly energized. At reception he asked if there were any rooms available. The girl behind the counter laughed and blushed.

Are you kidding? You practically have your pick, she said.

Magda and the Ear worked on next week's schedule.

This has to change. I'm too busy four of the five days. And I have nothing on Tuesday. I might as well not work on Tuesdays.

That would be best, said Magda.

Larry chatted with Tom in the lobby. Tom didn't know anything about the Great Gear announcement, but he did admit that his boss still hadn't arrived.

And there won't be any Great Gear without him. I can tell you that.

The airport reopened on Thursday night. The Ear told everyone to expect a flood of attendees. The conference could still be saved. Friday was all they needed. Sam knew no one was coming. Airlines and gear manufacturers don't work like that.

Oh, and be on the lookout for Lars, said the Ear. I want to know the moment he arrives.

Thursday's planned banquet for four hundred turned into an intimate all-you-can-eat lobster and filet mignon and pie feast for twenty. At the door Sobs distributed formal nametags for the dinner. The food kept coming and coming, relentlessly, like the storm the night before. Grant ate between Blair and Gwen.

At the same table the Ear ate between Magda and Rita. Larry ate with a salesman from Alabama who wheezed between forkfuls of food. Matt ate three entire lobsters. Sid challenged him to eat a fourth. Corey ate between Sobs and Tom, oblivious that he was a third wheel. Tyler dashed between tables seeing that everyone had everything they needed. Sam ate with the Florida contingent, telling them bad, old, bawdy jokes and half-true tales. Plate after full plate appeared from the kitchen. No one left hungry.

After the meal Cousin Dugong's was, almost literally, the only place to be. Blair and Grant and Gwen shared a round glass table. Sid and Tyler and Matt sat at another. Corey rested his elbows on the bar. Rita read in a corner. Sam sat at a bamboo table drinking with two marketing directors from Georgia. They told jokes and slapped crude nametags on one another. They grew louder and louder with every round and every passing hour. Matt wished he knew Finnish.

The Ear made a cameo appearance.

Has anyone heard anything from Lars? He's no longer returning my calls. Any deliveries?

Two of Cousin Dugong's customers mumbled no, most ignored the question, one snickered and two laughed outright. The Ear stomped off to his room. He hated barrooms and disrespect. Unbelievers. They'll see, he thought. They will see.

Soon nametags were everywhere: on bartenders, wait staff, attendees, tables, AGE employees, doors, chairs, curtains, beer bottles, floors, windows and railings, the Merry Manatee himself wore many. Hotel staff wore nametags on their nametags. Some of the nametags had actual names, most had nicknames or quotes, others had full sentences or short paragraphs. Some were rude, coarse and funny. Others were sweet and clever. Some were illegible. Nametags were everywhere amid the drinking. Cousin Dugong's was transformed by fermented words.

The time had come. They both knew it. But Tom and Sobs needed privacy, a location where they could be alone, a place they wouldn't be seen or interrupted. Tom held a key to Gearkegaard's unused room. It seemed the perfect solution.

While Sobs waited, sitting uncomfortably on the bed before moving to the lone chair, Tom went down to the bar and ordered drinks—two small light beers. Sobs was technically underage and Tom was nervous. Corey called to him, but Tom pretended he didn't hear. He was on a mission. Tom returned to the room wearing a nametag that said 'chicken'. Sobs snatched a pen from the desk and scribbled 'me too' on hers.

Larry was anxious in his room. He felt he should be doing something. He felt he should be proactive. As soon as I am done with the book, he told himself. And he started to finish the remaining twenty pages of *Detective, Detective*.

Gwen wouldn't or couldn't keep her hands off Grant.
Do you work out? You must work out. Ooh.

In between sips of her T&T Blair pretended not to care. Grant was gracious and enjoyed the company of the two attractive women. But he sensed that Blair was upset. He felt he owed her more. Grant grew tired, but he had work to do.

Ladies, this has been lovely, but I've been driving all day and it's time for me to call it a night.

Oh, no, said Gwen, one more drink. Please? For me?

Well—

Gwen hollered for the waiter to bring another round

Not for me, Gwen, said Blair. It's late. I am tired too.

Grant stood.

It was nice seeing you again.

You too.

Gwen yanked on Grant's belt and he plopped into his chair. She pushed a fresh drink over.

Tyler slurped the last drop of his fifth different cocktail, each chaperoned by a different colored umbrella. It was Sid's turn to pick.

Your next drink will be . . . a mai tai.

Tasty.

What color do you think the umbrella will be?

I love you conference guys, said Matt. You guys are the greatest. My turn next.

Grant took two quick sips of his Dewar's before apologizing to Gwen.

I really am very tired. I'm afraid I must be going.

153

Please stay.

I'm sorry. I can't. I really can't.

Gwen was deflated. She figured he was running off to Blair. She had lost.

Sweet dreams, she said.

Thanks. You too.

Gwen picked up her sweating rocks glass and moved to the bar.

Gearkegaard's reserved room, number 512, was on the fifth floor overlooking the beach. Sobs and Tom nursed warm beer watching faraway lightning flashes reveal black and gray cauliflower clouds. Neither spoke much. They were content being together.

Larry was in room 501. He finished the book and dropped it in the small trash can by the bed. The narrator-detective investigating the murder turned out to be the murderer. Larry became an agent. He listened as the door locked behind him. Then he tip-toed toward room 512.

Grant got off on the fifth floor, turned left and marched toward room 512.

Larry didn't know what he'd do at room 512. He thought it best to knock. If no one answered he'd go to bed.

If the room was empty Grant planned to let himself in and take a quick look around. Great Gear information might be hiding in plain sight.

Larry and Grant passed each other in front of Gearkegaard's room. They exchanged a quick 'good evening' and continued on their way. Neither slowed. Neither recognized the other.

A minute later, on the second pass, they tried to cover the coincidence with similar cover stories, little believable lies about forgetting something in the opposite direction. This time the opposing faces looked familiar.

The third time they met at room 512 a proper meeting became unavoidable. The sequence of events had become preposterous. They stopped. Inside, unheard and oblivious, Tom and Sobs shared a first kiss.

Do I know you?

You look familiar.

I thought I'd see if Lars was in his room.

Me too.

Grant knocked on the door. Tom bumped into the bed turning off the light.

California.

The Chang Affair.

Are you still with the State Department?

Still with Raygon?

Truthfully, one spy answered no and one answered yes.

Grant knocked harder.

Someone's in there. I heard something.

The light was on earlier.

Grant pounded.

Tom opened the door and launched into an apology. Grant cut him off and asked to see Lars Kilgore.

He's not here. He's not here yet. He's not even in Florida as far as I know.

The spies spied Sobs hiding in the shadows. They

apologized for the intrusion. Tom shut the door.

I imagine that we will again meet in another twenty-five years, said Larry.

I imagine that I'll see you tomorrow at the big announcement, said Grant.

Only through harmony can there be meaning in chaos.

A compromise between right and wrong is always wrong.

Good night, then.

Good night.

Early Friday in the darkness before dawn they awoke naked and face to face. Shaking off sleep and surprise they both blinked. He flipped over, stifled a scream and spoke first.

Oh my God, what did I . . . what have I done?

Morning, lover.

Oh my God! Oh my good God in heaven! This never happened. Do you hear me? This never happened. We never speak of this, do you hear me? We tell no one. Not a soul.

That's the thanks I get? You are quite the gentleman. Well, given your performance I can certainly understand why you wouldn't want anyone to know. Go on, then, get out. You're in my room.

And like the wind Corey gathered his pants and shirt and fled Gwen's hotel room undressed.

Friday's lunch established that everyone at the Merry Manatee was fed up with steak and lobster. The Ear still preached that the afternoon announcement would save the conference. He still expected people to arrive. All part of the Lord's plan, he told himself. But Gearkegaard was running out of time. And the Ear was praying for a miracle, one more miracle.

But the miracle did not occur. God did not intervene. Gearkegaard did not arrive in the nick of time. There were no late heroics. No packages arrived. But the show did go on. The Ear was far too invested to cancel the event. Wisely, however, he scrapped the scheduled live broadcast.

The Ear took the stage and the microphone in front of an audience of twenty-two: twelve from AGE, Grant, a couple of salesmen from Florida, Larry, the two marketing directors from Georgia, three hotel staff and a teenaged stringer from the *Buffett Island Weekly*.

This was supposed to be, he began, flashing a big white false smile, this was supposed to be a historic occasion. I did everything that was asked. I had faith. It was not supposed to end like this. And the worst part is that I don't know what happened. I don't know what went wrong. I don't know what comes next. The Great Gear exists. I know this despite all. It's true that I've never seen it, but I know it exists. Siddhartha, come up here. Please come up here and explain how the Great Gear exists.

Sid reluctantly took the microphone. The Ear left the stage and slumped into the nearest chair.

Hypothetically, said Sid, a simple transmission created from new metamaterials combining—no, sorry, I can't do this. I never believed in this super gear. I never thought it existed. I never, not for one second, believed that it could ever exist. I'm sorry. I can't help you.

As Sid left the stage Matt turned to Tyler and asked if he could transfer to conferences.

You guys are insane. Is it always like this?

No one moved. No one spoke. Then Tom stood and took the stage.

Rita watched in mild horror wondering how she would ever be able to spin this non-conference/non-event.

Tom began slowly, warily.

Most of you know me. I'm an engineer. I work with Siddhartha. I admire him. I respect him. He is very funny. He is also very honest. And, while it's true that I haven't seen the Great Gear either, that doesn't mean it doesn't exist, or can't exist. Gearke—Lars Kilgore is a genius and a man of integrity and if he says there's a Great Gear, well, that's good enough for me. Just because it failed to appear today on this stage like we all wanted it to doesn't mean we should give up on the idea. We should never let a little doubt be the difference between yes and no, between believing or not. We should never lose our ability to hope. Shouldn't we always be striving for the ideal, hoping one day to find it? Otherwise what's the point? At least that's what I think. I don't know. That's it, I guess. That's all I wanted to say.

Sobs felt a pinch of pride. Pluck, she thought, that's the word. And when he was done with what he wanted to say she clapped. The others joined her.

No one was happy packing. Most, however, were happy to be leaving. The Ear was the first to go. Magda momentarily misplaced one of her tiny bat bones. Corey didn't even try to retrieve his socks from Gwen's room. Blair was disappointed that Grant had left without saying good-bye. Sam bid adieu to the Merry Manatee and Cousin Dugong's by ordering a large whiskey in a to-go cup.

At the airport desk Tom and Sobs requested adjoining seats. As they waited to board Tom spoke about the night before.

It was amazing. You are amazing.

Tom, we didn't even do anything.

That's where you're wrong.

It was one kiss. It was nothing.

For me that was everything.

Oh, then you ain't seen nothin' yet, said Sobs taking his hand.

The big silver plane lifted into blue sky. While no one was looking the rain had stopped.

BROKEN TEETH

What I'm trying to convey to you doctor is that it was impossible to see who it was. It was dark. It was the middle of the night. I was half-conscious, confused. I was not at all in my right mind. At the time I was incapable of discernment. A moment earlier I had been in a deep sleep. It was an unfortunate accident. Yes, I am aware that this is the exact opposite of not harming myself or others. It is most distressing. My sympathies go out to my victim but you must understand that this is traumatizing for me as well. I am not nor have I ever been a violent man. Yes, until last night.

Who remembers the beginning of a dream or in this case a nightmare? One suddenly finds oneself plunged into the action, in media res, as it were. I was unconscious. In my dream state, that dream world, Gearkegaard and I were conversing, here in the hospital in my private room, he seated in the bedside chair and I propped up with pillows on the bed. We were just talking. It felt very normal. It was as if he had come for a friendly visit. He asked me how I'd been and whether I felt better. He may have tried to joke once or twice in that odd manner of his. We engaged in chit-chat. We spoke of mutual acquaintances and colleagues. We spoke of gears. At one point—and this is where the dream started to become unsettling, where it transmogrified and turned into a nightmare—Gearkegaard began discussing the perfect gear. I can't recall if it was he or I who mentioned it first, but I clearly recall asking to see it. It became imperative that I see it and hold it in my hand. He told me that that was impossible. He didn't have the perfect gear. He uttered one of his cryptic phrases: *a man of genius cannot remain spotless.* I was unable to decipher whether he lost the gear or it was stolen from him or he had never had it in the first place. He just kept repeating that he couldn't show it to me because he didn't have it. I became quite agitated. In fact I became irate. But I saw it! I screamed. I know it exists! You showed it to me! Gearkegaard just laughed. Then he sneered and said it was clear that I was suffering from a taste of omniscience. For some reason this made me angrier. He laughed louder. And it was then I am ashamed to admit that I became physical. I hurled myself at Gearkegaard in an attempt to stop his awful laughter and beat the truth out of him.

How was I to know that a fellow patient had wandered into my room in the dead of night? Aren't there restrictions on such nocturnal prowling? He must have come in on cat's paws, like a thief. How long was he sitting there I wonder. I was half asleep. In that horrible instant I was firmly convinced that he was Gearkegaard. You must see that it was all a terrible misunderstanding, an unfortunate intersection of fact and fiction. Furthermore the coincidence of his physiognomy was certainly a contributory factor, short and soft just like Gearkegaard himself. Despite my assault the poor man never called for help. He never once shouted stop. I may have been battling a pillow for all the resistance.

And now you report that he has a badly bruised face and a possible broken nose. But he will recover fully from his injuries, won't he? I am truly sorry. I don't know what else to say. It was a sickening misunderstanding.

Might such a vivid dream be a side effect of the tablets? Could this be the beginning of another bout of madness? Either way perhaps a dosage readjustment is in order. I shudder at the thought of a recurrence. Look at me. I am still shaking. I have endured hour after hour of prolonged shivering; I feel as though I am dripping with sweat. I am frightened. Doctor, I was in no position to discern where dream ended and reality began. And that is the awful truth.

Not that I am aware of, no. My parents always maintained that there had been an episode of sleepwalking at the age of ten—I allegedly urinated in a hall closet—but I have no recollection of the event. And there was no recorded repeat performance. Perhaps that is not surprising. Bleary confusion and disorientation—particularly upon awaking from a deep sleep—may indeed be common on the outside too; however, the level of scrutiny and the need for explanation are far greater within these walls. And what about the violence?

Yes, this incident will delay my release, I understand that much. It is to be expected. I had a premonition—though you know I do not believe in such nonsense—that the phrase *barring any setbacks* once uttered would subvert my chance for freedom. And it has come to pass. I was very close, wasn't I? Perhaps a day or two more and I would have gained my release. I would have been out on my own. I had begun to see the contours of the outside world in my mind's eye. I had begun to plan. So, yes, of course I am disappointed. I am disappointed and angry. I hope we can both agree that this is a normal healthy psychological reaction to the frustration of having my stay here extended.

Presently I am more angry than disappointed. Again, at this early stage, perhaps this is typical. What am I feeling? What does my anger *feel* like? Doctor I realize that you say certain things just to get me to react but banality is beneath you. I thought we were past such unoriginality. Yes, fine, I will indulge you, it feels, I *feel* like the figure in Edvard Munch's *The Scream*. The agony on his face is mine. The primal suffering under those orange clouds of blood is mine. The scream running through nature runs through me. *Unduly* dramatic? This is my freedom—my very life— that we are talking about, I believe I have the right to be dramatic. I believe I do. *The Scream* as a depiction of Depersonalization Disorder? See, that is the problem with you psychiatrists and your so-called

DSM, you feel the need to name everything. That's the way it is with you, you come across something you do not understand, perhaps it even scares you, and you give it a name and then it is a pet. You attempt to domesticate everything through nomenclature. Not everything has a name, doctor. This is the reason beauty and art exist. We will never understand everything. Were you aware that Munch's sister was an asylum patient at the time the painting was created? The asylum was located at the bottom of the hill in the picture. There was also a slaughterhouse nearby. You see the work boils with physical and emotional suffering. Yes, I am rather fond of Expressionism. If that makes me old-fashioned so be it. We all have our preferences. Munch once wrote in his notebook that it is not the chair which is to be painted but what the human being feels in relation to it. Yes, I thought that would appeal to your sensibilities. Our conversation is beginning to feel like a classroom. We are becoming professorial. I dislike such pedantry. I don't think either one of us is drawing any refreshment from these ridiculous speculations. And I am beginning to tire.

Let me attempt to describe my *feelings* in another way. Have you ever feared blindness? I am too blunt. Have you ever—after being in a very dark room for an extended period—opened your eyes and for a split second thought you had gone blind? That moment, that hesitation, that suspension, just before your eyes begin to adjust to the blackness and define shapes, that moment of fear and doubt that maybe this time your eyes will not adjust, that they will fail and you will forever be blind. Have you ever experienced this? Now imagine such a moment lasting a lifetime and instead of blindness it is your existence at stake. This is how I feel. And, yes, it is that dramatic.

If protocol dictates I am to be placed in isolation for a time then I suppose there is little left to say. Like a cooperative inmate I must accept my punishment. How else should I think of it? It seems as though everything is done for the protection of myself and others. At any rate I look forward to the peace and quiet and this I presume would also reduce the risk of future uninvited elfin night visitors. Yes, literally a small joke. Seriously, I do hope the poor man recovers from the injuries rapidly. And there are no professional concerns that solitary confinement might aggravate my condition. Ah, more medication. Perhaps the addition of another agent might inadvertently alleviate the dyspepsia. And does protocol also state how long I am to remain in isolation? Yes, I suppose every case is unique. We are all unique and we must all be protected. We humans are a complicated species. Although I tell myself, or at least try to tell myself that I value being alone, I must acknowledge that a part of me will miss the group sessions and my daily discussions with Doolittle. I feel as though I should say farewell. That is not allowed, I understand.

Alone at least I will have the time to contemplate the message of my Gearkegaard dream. Such a graphic and powerful experience demands inquiry. Certainly—the unfortunate assault notwithstanding— the nightmare is germane to my condition. It must reveal something. My initial reaction is that my mind is again searching for meaning. Gearkegaard's oneiric visitation is an indisputable sign of recovery. There can be no other possible explanation. What would Gearkegaard make of all this I wonder. He is a very wise man doctor, a very wise man. He is a man of science who understands that rationalism can carry us only so far. I can't help but wonder what project currently engages him. Has he moved beyond his perfect gear? Perhaps he has built a working model. Perhaps the perfect gear is already in production. Such momentous news surely would have made its way here, even to this godforsaken place. What if the gear doesn't exist? What if it never existed? What if, through the prism of my inceptive madness, I imagined the perfect gear? Perception is, of course, a creative act involving not only one's senses but also one's emotions and expectations, a so-called rubber ruler. What if I misperceived what Gearkegaard brought to me? And what if that misperception has become part of my memory, thus affecting new perceptions and interpretations? After all it has been months since I saw Gearkegaard's plans. How much do I accurately remember? But why am I speculating in this manner? Why am I second-guessing myself? I now doubt because of one silly dream? No, the gear is real and that is that. How do I know it's real? I just do. Call it whatever you want. For lack of a better term let's call it faith: faith in my memory, faith in Gearkegaard, faith in my own abilities, faith in my sanity. It doesn't matter. I just know. You do not believe me. You do not believe there is a perfect gear.

I see that you are trying to hide your smile. You don't even believe there is a Gearkegaard, do you? Oh, that's absurd. It is a silly nickname. His real name is Lars, Lars Kilgore. I'm sure I could produce him if my future depended on it.

Yes, I speak of him with respect. He is a fine and talented man. Would I be angry if the very real Gearkegaard were standing before me? Impossible, that would be like being angry with Santa Claus. Would I—do I?—blame him for my illness? You are provoking me to no end. It would be ludicrous to blame Gearkegaard for anything. It would be comparable to blaming nature for a hurricane. It's nonsensical, like my nightmare. Yes, that is one of the more vexing aspects of this experience. Why would I want to hurt Gearkegaard? Why, indeed.

In fact I imagine a reunion with Gearkegaard would be most pleasant. There was never any animosity between us. And it would be nice I dare say to see a familiar face. He would be extremely cordial, as always. He would ask after my health and my family. I imagine the conversation would be somewhat emotional for me, particularly with everything that has transpired. I feel that my natural reserve would be tested by my curiosity. I couldn't help but ask—earlier than prescribed by decorum—about the gear. I can hardly conceive what his answer might be. Ah, doctor, I feel I have left a profession that is totally ruined, one to which I can never return.

Yes, of course I am still disturbed. And I am tired. And I am sick. Yes, my digestive troubles continue to plague me, but I am referring to another sickness, not one of the bowels or one of insanity. I do not know how to describe it. Maybe it is simply a profound boredom. To be frank, doctor, I am not certain how much longer I will be able to tolerate any more of this miserable comedy. I dislike it here. I am well enough to go home. Anything else is torture. Tell me, doctor, is there some conclusive way to know when I can be released? Is there anything I can do to accelerate the process? I am quite tired of being here. I am tired of talking. I will be released soon, won't I? Whatever you do please never tell me that my stay here has become indefinite. I would not be capable of processing such a future. How can there be people who find it possible to exist in a place like this? How are they able to continue? I suppose like everywhere else one becomes blinded to its horrors by daily familiarity. We all merely do the best we can, moment after monotonous moment. Doctor, I fear most of all that there will come a time in which I will no longer believe in my release. And this inability to believe will render these discussions, my monologues, largely pointless, and I shall close up like a clam to be alone with my diseased thoughts like all the others doomed to remain here until dead. I am tired and afraid.

Yes, I am ready for the nurse—nurse in name only, of course—to show me back to my cell. If nothing else I could use the rest, anything to stop this dreadful torrent of words.

THE GREAT GEAR

The Ear kept his job. That in itself was a lesson in thaumatology. Beyond the insular gear manufacturing world, the conference disaster made no splash. Mary had made all the news. In addition, AGE's executive committee feared admitting a major hiring mistake. A man cannot be blamed for a hurricane, they said. And the Great Gear may yet surface, they hoped. He was saved. And so the Ear continued as if everything that had happened was preordained. He stayed the course. He kept to the plan. His faith remained resolute.

There's always a traitor among us, Magda, said the Ear. The Bible tells us so. Never forget that. When he gets here, please send him in immediately. No need to prolong this.

Sam was always in good spirits after returning from a conference. Being with others energized him. Despite the debacle, he felt rejuvenated, younger. He bounced. Magda sent him bouncing in to the Ear without looking up from the Acropolis screensaver displayed on her monitor.

Behind his big desk the Ear opened a fat folder.

Take a seat, Sam.

Sam sat. The Ear pushed forward a performance review. Sam took it but didn't read.

When I started here, said the Ear, I was quite clear—crystal clear, I thought—that this was a new AGE, an AGE of measurement and accountability. I was clear, was I not? You understood that, I hope?

Yes, you were. And, yes, I did.

Good. Good. In your hands is an objective performance assessment. It, however, is not very good.

I wouldn't think so, what with the—

Not good at all. In fact, it is horrid.

Sure, the circumstances were a bit weird. It was most definitely the strangest conference we've ever had. I'll give you that.

Sam, you don't get it.

Get what?

I'm sorry. I'm going to have to let you go. Your performance, by any measure, is unacceptable. You have it before you in black and white.

It was one conference and it was because of the weather, said Sam.

It was not the weather. I told you to have faith, answered the Ear.

You're blaming me for a hurricane? I'm being fired because of a storm?

No, you are being *let go* because you failed to meet your minimum goals, any of them. This is not about the weather. This is about results. This is about locus of control. It's called taking responsibility.

It's called covering your ass, thought Sam.

Imagine if one of our members built a gear that didn't do the job. Imagine no matter what they did it wouldn't work. What do you do? You don't keep trying. You get another one. You replace it with one that works, said the Ear. Sam had stopped listening.

Rita quit typing. She was working on yet another press release about the Great Gear. She found it difficult to write about something that she'd never seen and didn't understand. It felt fictitious. Her thoughts wandered to her never-ending novel-in-progress. Was it really true that she'd been working on it for nearly ten years? All the late nights, all the weekends, all the writing and rewriting, plotting and planning. She was currently entertaining a new idea that the book's beginning might be stronger if the lovers-to-be first met during a category five hurricane in the nation's capital. That would punch up the opening, she thought. Ten years and I'm still working on the beginning. Sometimes I don't think I'll ever be finished, she thought.

What are you doing? asked Sobs.

Packing up. What's it look like? Been turned out on my ear. Sorry, not funny. I've been canned. After twenty years, can you believe it? Apparently our ghost conference wasn't what he envisioned. Seems I'm not new AGE material. You're safe, though he didn't much like your nametags. I told him Tyler would be an able replacement. Don't know if that'll help or hurt him. I did what I could. You hang in there, kid. Remember, it's just a job. Don't worry about me. I'll be fine. Take care of yourself.

Out of character, Gearkegaard was garrulous.

I do not know what happened. They were ready. I held them in my hands. They were beautiful. One was smaller than my fingernail. It was stunning. It was perfect. It fit in my palm. You'd hardly know it was there. It was incredible. Imagine a silent drone the size of a mosquito. The second transmission was much larger, but I wanted to prove the design was scalable. They were both so beautiful.

The Ear considered Gearkegaard and thought he looked smaller than normal, as if he were being swallowed by the chair, word by word.

Okay, one last time, for the record, let's go through the series of events, step by step, as you remember them. Okay? Okay.

I have told you, began Gearkegaard, I had both prototypes ready to go. I'd even tested them with rudimentary motors at the lab. Everything was fine. There was still time. I packed them carefully, called the delivery service, they came and picked up the package, and then I went to the airport.

What happened next?

I was unable to get a flight to Florida.

The package never arrived, said the Ear.

So you have informed me.

The delivery service has no record of the shipment.

So they say.

Let me ask you this. Why didn't you carry the little one, the one that fit in your hand? Why ship it?

I wanted them both to arrive in time for the announcement. I thought a package had a better chance of making it. I feared I would not be able to catch a flight.

Okay, what did you do after the airport?

I realized that I had left my phone and notes at the university lab so I went back.

And?

And, they were not there. Nothing was there. All my documents, all the computers, everything was gone.

Did you call the police?

No, I went to the engineering department chair and told him what had happened. I asked him if they'd moved my things. He made a call and then said that all university property was accounted for and that he wasn't responsible for my missing items. He offered to call university police if I wished.

Is that true?

Yes, he offered to call.

No, I mean is it true that the university wasn't responsible for your things in his lab.

Yes, that was one of the stipulations in our agreement.

What did you do next?

I went home.

You didn't call the police?

No. I thought I had, maybe, misplaced my things. The last few months have been hectic. I had been working so much that I thought I might be wrong, that I might not be remembering correctly. So I went home.

And what did you do at home?

I tried to call you but couldn't get through. The line wasn't working. I thought that was odd.

And were your missing items there?

No.

And were they at the office?

No, there were not.

You understand, don't you, that everything you've developed, no matter where it is, belongs to AGE. It is proprietary information.

I would humbly submit that such ideas belong to humanity. It belongs to everyone.

Perhaps, but in this case by AGE's grace.

Mm.

The two men who picked up the package, what did they look like?

They looked like deliverymen.

Nothing unusual about them?

No, not that I noticed. I was rushing.

So, to summarize, you want me to believe that the Great Gear exists, or at least existed, in two separate prototypes, and these were carried off by two unknown men. And we don't know where they are now, the gears or the men. Furthermore, you claim that everything related to the development of the gear, all the plans, the schematics, files and drives, equipment, drawings, everything, has mysteriously disappeared. Do I have it about right?

Yes, that is what happened.

It's a pretty unbelievable story, don't you think?

It is what happened.

Yes, so you say.

I could, I suppose, do it all over again, said Gearkegaard, recreate them. It would take time. I have the designs in my head. But I do not know if I have the heart.

The Ear flashed his ivory teeth.

I understand. And I thank you. There'll be no need for that. You have done your best. Your part is over.

The Ear stood and cleared his throat.

Your story is unbelievable. That much is most certainly true. You easily could have concocted this absurd account. On the other hand you could have concocted a more plausible one. But, the bottom line is that I believe you. I believe you because it is absurd.

Gearkegaard appeared to grow a bit or else it was the chair disgorging him, thought the Ear.

And do you want to know why I believe you? It's because I know the Lord works in mysterious ways, that's why. Nothing is too absurd for God. I know it from personal experience.

The Ear sat down close to Gearkegaard.

When I was younger—mid-twenties, seems a lifetime ago—I wasn't the man you see today. I was reckless, arrogant and selfish. I didn't believe in anything but myself. I was not a nice person. I did bad things, horrible things. One afternoon, after doing another terrible thing, I was racing through the streets on a motorcycle, drunk, weaving in and out of traffic like I was playing a video game. I didn't think about anybody else. I didn't think about dying or about my mortality. I thought I was invincible. I was, of course, wrong. I died that afternoon, Lars. Yes, I did. A truck pulled out in front of me and I couldn't swerve or stop. I ditched the bike and slid underneath the semi and everything went black. The next moment I was floating, suspended by a warm light, looking down at my own mangled lifeless body. One of the EMTs said *He's gone* but I didn't feel anything. I wasn't sad or angry. I was at peace. The light grew brighter but softer and a divine voice told me that it wasn't my time. I heard Christ's voice. I was born . . . again. I was saved. I returned to my body. I will never forget that moment. I can still feel that warm light. Every time I run my tongue over these false front teeth I remember that I died that day. Every time I think about having a drink I remember that voice of salvation. He commanded me to live. He gave me a second chance. And I've been listening to Him ever since. His is the voice of the Great Gear. That's how I know it's real. That's how I know your story is real. The Lord wants us to remember. He wants us to believe. And that's why I believe you.

Fallibility is what makes memory, said a larger, recomposed Gearkegaard.

And we are all fallible, said the Ear. Perfection exists only in God, not in man. I remember my sins too. I'm sure you remember yours. But your part in the Great Gear story is over. We live in the real world after all, not paradise. Mistakes have been made. There are ramifications. You know what that means don't you?

Through the Ear's artificial smile Gearkegaard saw that he was being asked to resign. His time at AGE had ended.

Thank you, Lars. His work will go on. All will be revealed. In time. All in His good time.

Tom waited for Gearkegaard to exit the Ear's office. This was the second time in less than a year that he expected his boss to be fired. Magda was half hidden behind her desk unthinkingly rubbing her deep blue *mati*. The door opened. Gearkegaard's face told Tom the worst had happened.

There's something mystical in the proud man, said Gearkegaard.

Tom had no idea what Gearkegaard was talking about.

When Sid learned that Sam had been fired and Gearkegaard had been forced out he was incensed. In a personal *auto de fé* he pronounced the Ear pure evil. He came up with what he thought was a perfect new nickname for the Ear. Torquemada. The bit-too-clever sobriquet did not catch on.

Larry loathed most contemporary music. It sounded like caterwauling. It lacked beauty, subtlety. But Peggy was the musician in the house and she had selected the song. This year the girls will sing *California Girl* by the Candy Butchers, she announced as if it would mean something to him. His two girls had been singing together—with one voice, he'd always thought—since they could speak. Now grown, the girls—the young women—begrudgingly consented to perform at the Laurel Neighbors Association's annual talent show.

Peggy played the piano. Larry listened. The girls' voices have equally matured over the years, he thought. Richer, fuller, but still balanced. Hannah Yang Guang, the elder, as she always did, assumed the lead. Samantha Yu, the younger, had had enough. She stopped.

Why does Hannah always get the good part?

Sam, one part is no better than the other. You sing together, in harmony, said Peggy.

Not this time, said Samantha storming off.

Larry waved off Peggy and hurried after his youngest child.

He caught up to her in her old room.

I know it's ridiculous, Dad. It's meaningless. But I'm always second.

It is not meaningless, said Larry. It is life. But we all have to work together. We all must play our role.

Why is my role not the lead?

I do not know. Some questions have no answers. But there is a saying that the wise save the best for last.

Is that a bit of ancient Chinese wisdom?

It is from an adult diaper advertisement.

Did you know that the frigate bird, despite spending most of its time over water, can't dive? asked the senator.

Grant grunted that he was unaware of the fact.

Incredible, isn't it? They live along the coast; they eat fish, but they can't get their feathers wet. Really.

Their feathers, believe it or not, are uncoated and non-water-resistant. You know what happens if they get wet? They can't fly. The feathers get bogged down. It makes the bird too heavy to take off again. They would be sitting frigate birds. They would die. Yet they eat only fish. Amazing. So, how do they get their fish, you ask? Well, if it wants to eat, the frigate bird has to harass other seabirds, pecking at them, yanking their tales in midair—the frigate bird is an excellent flyer—doing whatever it takes until the harassed bird regurgitates, throws up, any fish just caught. The frigate bird snatches the vomited meal out of the air and flies off to eat, feathers still dry. Amazing, isn't it? There's more than one way to skin a cat, Grant, remember that.

Yes, sir. I won't forget.

The instant Tom picked up the telephone he regretted it. A telemarketer's voice asked if he was engineer Tom Healy. Tom thought about hanging up but he didn't want to be rude.

Yes, this is Tom Healy.

The voice claimed it was coming from a headhunter—senior corporate recruiter, actually— and would Tom be interested in hearing about an interesting opportunity.

Before Tom could answer the voice continued.

It's an exciting opportunity. They have requested you by name. This is highly unusual. They must really want you. And this means that you are in a very profitable position. It is quite a jump from where you're at now, literally. It's in California. It's a firm called Raygon. I'm sure you are familiar with them. Don't say anything at this stage. Let me send you the information I have and I'll be in touch. Look over the offer. Remember there's always room for negotiation. I'll be in touch in a few days. Thank you for your time, Tom. I look forward to our next conversation.

Tom was in shock. He felt he'd been hit by a lightning bolt. Corey walked by and told him to close his mouth.

Shut your trap. Nobody wants to see what's inside, Corey laughed.

The gentleman I had known as Live4Seduction turned out to be a twice divorced claims adjustor named Brad, said Gwen.

But you've been divorced twice too, said Sobs.

First of all it's different for women. And, second, the guy's idea of seduction was all-you-can-eat breadsticks at the Olive Garden followed by a bad box of wine back at his place.

Oh.

I'm done with this online dating. I've had it. It's all phony. From now on I'll get my men the old-fashioned way: cleavage and simulated caring.

Tyler was promoted to director of conference services. He seized the opportunity. He reorganized the department. He arrived early and worked late. He moved files and rearranged the furniture. He made phone calls. He crafted complex conference goals. Sobs kept her job. But Tyler told her that in the future she would have to be more decisive if she wanted to be successful. Matt applied for the open position on the team unaware that the team was not what it once was.

I am sorry I didn't get to say good-bye the last time. I was unexpectedly called away, said Grant. The senator—

You don't owe me an explanation, said Blair.

No, but I would appreciate it if you accepted my apology anyway. I don't want you thinking I'm someone I'm not.

Okay, you are forgiven.

Thank you. That is kind. Oh, one more thing. I met up with an old friend who works on K Street. All types of clients. Hands in everything. He mentioned that he was looking for good people. I dropped your name. I hope you don't mind. Don't worry. It's not like I committed you. In fact, I said that I hadn't the faintest idea if you'd be interested, just that you are talented. He said he'd love to hear from you. Said you might be precisely the person he's looking for. I'll send you his information. No pressure. Call or don't. It's up to you.

Thank you. It's my turn to say that is kind.

My pleasure. Just do me a favor. If you make it to D.C. give me a call.

Blair thanked Grant a second time and put down the phone. She wondered how quickly she could call without seeming desperate.

Tom thought the offer was too good to be true. It was like he was dreaming. It was hard to believe. He couldn't wrap his head around it. He had to talk it over with somebody.

Would you come with me to California? he asked Sobs.

What?

Tom explained the offer. He told her that it was perfect. He had to take it. He had no choice. She agreed. But he wanted her to be with him. He wanted her to be with him always, forever.

It's too fast. It doesn't make sense. You're not being logical.

Love should come before logic, said Tom.

On Gearkegaard's last day Tom placed a round, white, store-bought cake in the center of the break room table. He opened a wide drawer and grabbed a fistful of plastic forks and a stack of pink paper plates that read 'Happy Birthday!' He didn't know what else to do. He thought someone had to do something to commemorate the diminutive man's great career. One by one downcast staff members arrived. No one, not even Blair, was glad the beloved engineer was leaving. The Ear came with a prepared speech. They waited before cutting the cake. Gearkegaard did not show. It was just as well. No one felt like celebrating anyway. The cake, however, did not go uneaten.

A SIMPLE TRANSMISSION

You speak as if I should be grateful that I am no longer consigned to my room, as if the end of isolation were something to be celebrated, that I should be happy or honored, like it was my birthday. Nonsense, it was nothing but an arbitrary sanction for an accidental crime. I am fed up with the fake breakthroughs and illusory progress. I'm not so mad as to fall for what is patently absurd. And I recognize that your brand of quasi-freedom is merely another illusion.

I enjoy the solitude or have you forgotten. Perhaps you now confuse me with your other patients; I am just another talking head. No, my sentence, the time alone, was a blessing in fact. I have never—at least in recent memory, that is—thought more clearly. And that is the unadulterated truth. Speaking of memory reminds me to share the big news. Yes, it is enormous news. While I was confined to my room and my thoughts Doolittle was released.

Isn't that amazing? My friend Doolittle is now somewhere on the outside undoubtedly conversing with cats or rats or dogs or harassing unsuspecting passersby. It is unbelievable, miraculous. I tell you doctor that man is as mad as a hatter. Maybe he belongs out there. But his escape seals my fate, doesn't it? No two men were ever more unalike. And if he is on the outside it stands to reason that I must remain on the inside. I will never get out. No, I am resigned to it. I have made my peace. We can dispense with the pretense. It is of little consequence. For if a man is labelled crazy, then he's crazy, and if he's let out and reprieved he's still crazy, because that's what he has been and he's only out of the straightjacket, and that's not the same as living and being like the rest. Either way there is no way for it to end but in dejection.

On a more practical note, however, with Doolittle gone I have become the resident pariah. The other inmates now go out of their way to avoid me. Group as you can well imagine has become an uncomfortable farce. I am shunned. You're the only one who looks me in the eyes anymore. It's a pity. I think they all see their own mortality and they are afraid to look. You aren't afraid. I know. That's because you're too young and preoccupied to know any better. You don't know enough to sense the end.

Yes, of course I am taking my medication. I am no doctor but I think the new tablet you've added to my palette of pills is most beneficial. It appears to have relieved my digestive issues which is a godsend. It is round and white, the combination of all the colors of the visible spectrum. Yes, I take it dutifully. Twice a day that little pearl of innocence is placed in my mouth and swallowed. I well understand that I couldn't exist without my pharmaceuticals. Believe it or not, doctor, I want to live and to go on living, even if it's contrary to the rules of logic.

Another rather meaningless thought dawned on me just now. I was born in the analog age and I shall die in the digital one. The world has changed. They are two very different eras, are they not? Human nature will in time adapt no doubt. But it must do so without me. No, I was a mere witness not a participant. I was but a witness to an *age of conversion*. Born analog to die digitally, yes, I find that amusing.

Years ago a man I knew at the university, a fellow engineer, died of a heart attack—myocardial infarction, you medical people call it—and I felt it incumbent to attend his funeral. You see we had been friendly at school—that was back when I had experimented with friendship and we had both been at the top of our class—and I, for one reason or another, wished to say good-bye to my former friend and rival. Robert had been a wonderful engineer with a supple mind. He took a very tactile approach to his exercises. He was always fixing something or other, turning greasy parts in his calloused hands. After receiving his undergraduate degree he skipped graduate school to work as a mechanic. We all thought he was throwing away his talent. But he elected to work with his hands. He followed his passion. Eventually he owned more than a dozen garages and ended his days quite wealthy. And up until the end he worked every day in the garage getting his hands dirty. He knew himself which is something not often said in describing most of us. By any measurement he had a good life. At the funeral— of course, I didn't know a soul—I paid my respects and shook hands with strangers. At one point I overheard a man—I do not know his relation to the deceased, but he was well-dressed and I would guess family—I overheard this man in conversation say of Robert *I've never seen him cleaner.* All this man could manage to say, the only words he could muster for the dead man, was that he was now clean, more presentable, like the rest of us I suppose. Now I fully understand that grief takes many forms but the stranger's words made me profoundly sad and also raises the question, what if anything will they say about me? Will they say CEO of yore goes crazy and dies in institution? And, more importantly, why do I care?

I do not care and maybe that's worse. In fact it might be the worst thing imaginable. I have had enough. I have allowed myself to be subjected to this demented interrogation for long enough. I am tired and I would like to be alone. Yes, but I don't have a choice in the matter, do I? Okay, I'll play a final psychological game, one last therapeutic exercise, okay doctor, I'll play. Make it a good one. Sure. Right now if I could be anywhere in the world I would like to be sitting in my favorite green armchair—it has a matching ottoman so I might put my feet up—and the armchair and ottoman would be placed in front of a painting at the National Gallery of Art in

Washington, D.C. There would be no one else there, just me and the painting. Oh, yes, the painting, of course you are curious. The painting would be the signature untitled piece from Mark Rothko's *Black on Gray* series. Yes, Abstract Expressionism. It is a magnificently simple piece: two large rectangles, one above the other, the lower one gray and the upper one black, surrounded by a white border. It first captures your attention by suggesting a moonscape, like you are standing on some desolate planet looking into a vast starless universe. But then the white border draws you closer and you realize that the black and gray are not as black and gray as you first thought. You are pulled closer by this discovery. The 'solid' black appears to be layered shades of varying blacks while the gray somehow contains hints of lavender and brown. And the brushstroke textures draw you closer and closer. You think you discern tantalizing lines suggesting shadows of shapes but they invariably disappear; it seems a commingling of the possible and the impossible, and you try to look deeper, squinting, but ultimately there's nothing to be seen, neither space nor substance, amid an impression of everything. It all dissolves into disorder. You are returned to infinity. Your journey leads you back to the void. I believe I could sit and gaze at that painting forever. That, doctor, is where I would like to be right now. And, since you asked, sitting in my own armchair with its matching ottoman would make all the difference in the world.

HARMONIC DRIVE

After a while it really began to look like a new AGE.
The great path forward was revised and relaunched.
Old faces were gone and new faces filled the short,
neutral-color-repainted corridors. The Ear hired the
nauseatingly named Chad Chadsworth, an old
acquaintance from StunTek, to be the director of the
rebranded Creative Design and Consulting Services
department. He was immediately put to work on the
Great Gear. The Ear, hedging his and the Lord's bets,
also contracted with a furtive private detective who
went by the name Ben Gerson to try and locate
Gearkegaard's missing prototypes and plans.

One new face was an old—though not too old—
face. Gwen had invested a sizeable chunk of her
savings on a series of minor surgical operations that
made her look timeless. I'm a new me, she exclaimed
delighted with the results. She was certain the physical
improvements would yield relationship results.

Magda continued to answer the Ear's telephone, keep his calendar and make his copies, but she was within a year of retirement and Greece beckoned. There was island light at the end of her nine-to-five tunnel. Although she had accrued enough vacation time to retire ahead of schedule, she instead elected a four day work week. Never again would she have to work another unlucky Tuesday. Now, the jinxed Tuesdays were spent amid idyllic dreams of brightly colored icons and whitewashed walls, meticulously preparing for her ineluctable relocation to the sundrenched Giannis homestead overlooking the Aegean.

Siddhartha didn't get on well with Chad Chadsworth. In a closed door meeting he told the Ear that his new director didn't measure up. He doesn't know the first thing about gear design, said Sid. He isn't one-fifth the engineer that Gearkegaard is. When the Ear refused to listen and sided with Chad, Sid announced that he had had it with the Ear and well-dressed, smiley, crazy people in general. He quit AGE and told Corey that he was going to try his hand and mouth at stand-up comedy.

Matt joined Tyler in conferences but didn't like it any better than lobbying. It was more work than he'd imagined. And they didn't drink nearly as much as he'd assumed. He was the grunt, just like before. Daily he thought about quitting, but he lacked Sid's courage.

Gwen got on with Chad, famously. She and her new

face began an energetic love affair with the slightly younger engineer. They appeared to be in love. She thought he was dreamy. He thought she was vivacious. They fit. And together they made each other happy.

As he had done so many times in the past Gearkegaard vanished without a trace. No one took much notice. Several months after his official last day at AGE he sent an email message to the entire staff, a single cryptic sentence. It read: Our obligation is to accept our beliefs as we have accepted the universe and our having been brought into it.

No one was quite sure what it meant. The Ear half-suspected it was code and forwarded it to Gerson for further analysis.

Senior Texas Senator Overton Archer was named the director of the Central Intelligence Agency. As his first order of business he had an aquarium of spitting fish installed in his new office. Despite this, Grant stayed with him.

When work permitted Grant and Blair met for dinner, usually someplace close to her K Street office. The last time they spoke she was representing the government of Cameroon. He, of course, could not discuss whatever it was that he did, though he did share one of Archer's animal stories: an unappetizing account of Mexican free-tail bats jamming rivals' echolocation signals in a survival-of-the-fittest battle for insects.

Rita finally finished her romantic novel, *The Cure for Crying*. Her love story had ended. The main characters found each other and pledged their eternal love. She thought it quite good. There wasn't a word to add, nothing to delete. It was complete. She was satisfied. It was done. She placed it on her shelf among books written by other people. She didn't have the stomach or the heart or any other organ's desire to send it to an agent or a publisher. It was to remain with her. She had been with the characters and their story for so long the book felt like a fictional childhood friend, a delusory memory she wanted to keep all to herself.

Corey had hoped to go to Washington with Blair. When that didn't happen he knew that he wouldn't be promoted into her position. He was too young, too inexperienced and lacked the necessary contacts. Not even the Ear was that brainless, he told himself. He worked to make it look like he was working as he awaited his new boss. Rumor had it that the new lobbying director was a former senator's staffer. He hoped it would be a woman. His charms worked better on women, he thought. Either way, he was confident he'd do well. He was confident in his future.

Without much effort Sam landed a new job. He was hired as corporate relations director at the Merry Manatee. It was less money, but the lifestyle was worth it. He became a Cousin Dugong's regular and an avid beachcomber. He found that he excelled at shelling. He even appeared on the front page of the local newspaper after he found a rare Junonia (*Scaphella junonia*). The black and white photograph captured contentment in Bermuda shorts and a Hawaiian shirt. Beaming, he held his arms aloft, the coveted spotted shell in one hand and a tall umbrella drink in the other. Sam sent the picture to all his old friends at AGE with the caption, 'Living the Dream.'

The Ear waited in his office for news of the Great Gear. He would wait forever if need be. He convinced himself the miracle would occur when least expected. He preached confidence and ran his tongue over his perfectly fabricated teeth. The Lord told him to be patient and he was patient. His faith sustained him.

Darryl Lawrence stopped speaking and remained in the hospital. The doctors fed him all kinds of magic pharmaceuticals trying to make him talk. Mostly he slept. Time passed and he often forgot who he was and why he was there. One day his sister, Karen, visited. He recognized her immediately. He asked her how she was and he asked about Heather. After she left the doctors told him that this was a sign he was getting better. But Darryl didn't feel any better or any worse. He didn't know what to believe.

And under a wide cloudless sky Tom and Sobs played with their puppies, Fides and Ratio, in the front yard. They were trying to teach the clumsy, creamy Labs their new names, but confusion reigned. They wrestled and rolled, laughed and yapped. Tongues wagged. The dry brittle lawn began to bake. The young couple had made no concession to the California sun. Cynical Sobs wore all black. Tom and his Irish complexion shunned sunscreen.

We should go inside, said Tom. The pups are getting thirsty. And I'm toasting.

You said the sun would be good for me, brighten my perspective.

Everything in moderation, said Tom. Besides, beliefs should evolve.

Just then a horn honked. A large car pulling a small trailer parked at the curb. Waving, they rose. Tom's new boss Larry had come to make their brown grass green.